ON THE RUN WITH MIKE AND GUNN

A THRILLER

JAMES LAWSON MOORE
"THE RENEGADE MILLENNIAL"

Cover Design: Ashanti Luke
Author Photo: Eric Cline
Formatting Assistance: Stephen H. King ("TOSK")

Sections of this novel appeared in early unedited form on the writing and community website Wattpad.

"Ghosts At The Door" appeared in a slightly different form on the author's personal blogsite—therenegademillennial.wordpress.com

This is a work of fiction. Names, characters, businesses, places, events, locales, and incidents are either the products of the author's imagination or used in a fictitious manner. Any resemblance to actual persons, living or dead, or actual events is purely coincidental.

FIRST EDITION
ISBN: 9781798430286

DEDICATION

To Jim Thompson, the poet laureate of the pulp thriller, the author of *The Grifters* and *The Killer Inside Me*, both of which have inspired me to write quickly and with the white hot center and the presence of mind to be free.

CONTENTS

Author's Note

About the Author

AUTHOR'S NOTE

It took me until I was 28 to write a novel.

Oh, I've written several starts to one over the years, starting with the 60 pages I completed in the eighth grade when I first consciously discovered writing. With that and every other attempt that came after I tried too hard to speak without the proper voice, to enact the beast with something other than the natural guttural roar that was already inside me. Pretentious and stupid, I was too dumb to know just how dumb I truly was. But now I can sleep peacefully knowing the depth of my own stupidity.

But now I have something tangible in my hands. A full length novel, just a hair under 50,000 words. It's short but good, if I do say so myself. Praise the Lord, and pass the potatoes.

I had some help along the way. My mom and dad, Janice Harris and the reverend Woody Carter Moore, pushed me to always be at my own creative best. The renegade sci-fi author/professor Ashanti Luke did me a solid and put together the groovy cover. The man known as "TOSK," or Stephen H. King, helped me with the formatting.

I hope you enjoy *On The Run With Mike and Gunn*. This will forever hold the distinction of being my first novel, and though I plan on writing another three or four novels in the next few years alone this baby will be my favorite child among them all.

At 28 it took me a little while to give birth to her. But I'm glad to mother her along all the same.

All best,

James Lawson Moore

PROLOGUE

25 years ago, in an orphanage somewhere in northern Virginia...

Even at 10 years old the kid knew he was too big to be playing around so rough with the other kids congregating around the back fields of the place. That was his blessing and his curse, and only Michael Liebowitz could own the fullness and the double face of that paradox. A mind that was as complex as the cosmos, fitted into a tank of a body—that was Michael, the boy giant.

None of the other kids could comprehend the sheer force of what they were dealing with when they first grouped together in the back yard of the orphanage, centering their attack toward the one common enemy they all shared. Like ants clawing their way after God, these were mere mortals, with no depth of understanding of what exactly they were up against.

They would know soon enough.

"All right kid," shouted the ringleader of the mob. A snaggle-toothed little pimply-face, going by the newly christened name of Elmore Johnson because the adults who ran the orphanage couldn't find his birth certificate (or any other identifying documents from when he was brought in), he grinned from ear to ear as he pointed an overly long

1

finger at the kid giant. "You know you can't be here anymore. We can't stand to have you hanging around. You're just too big; you eat too much and there's not enough food to split between half of us."

The boy giant looked Elmore dead in the eye, and stood there silently for several long moments. The more he stared, without so much as blinking or breathing visibly, the more Elmore in turn began shaking where he stood, at the front of his hoard.

Soft murmurings made their way through the crowd that stood behind their not-so-fearless leader. "Look at him," one voice whispered. "Watch how his eyes don't move," hushed another. And still another voice hummed, "Doesn't look like he's breathing at all..." Even as their leader and the boy giant who stood several yards away from him eyed each other in a solemn staring match, the hoard had already begun to lose its nerve, and in typical hive mind activity the other kids took several steps back so as to distance themselves from the faltering leader of the cause.

Elmer had begun to sweat as he stared down his foe; he frantically started to wipe the drops of water from his forehead as fought to raise his crackling voice back to its former authoritarian stature. "Just beat it kid, get lost. Go on, get out of here. Run away, join the circus, get hit by a train—we don't care what you do. We just don't want you here anymore, you freak."

As that last word was flung out into the air—*freak*, as in the chief freak of the backyard—the kid giant suddenly jumped to life. His eyes narrowed, and his fists clenched into solid blocks of unbridled power and rage. The air blowing out from the kid's nostrils was coming in so strongly that some of the members of the hoard would later swear that they saw the wind itself shake loose from out of his whole body.

Even at 10 years old, the kid knew he was too big to let this go on any further. But it was too late; what had been opened could not be closed again. Not without blood being spilled upon the tarnished ground.

The beatdown was so severe that it should have lasted only a few minutes. The boy giant moved so swiftly that it could hardly be said that he had moved at all, and once he reached Elmore he went straight to work. Fists came down hard, covering the lesser kid's back and face and body like chunks of hail covering the broad side of a barn roof in the middle of a storm. It was an unnatural act of aggression, the likes of which should not be in the possession of a 10 year old body—even one so monstrously big as this.

Half the hoard had dispersed the moment the first punch landed; the other half stayed and watched, partly in fascination and partly out of fear for their precious little world that was just now starting to come crumbling down. After several minutes went by, several minutes which should have been the sum total of the attack, some more murmurings were beginning to rumble through the crowd. "He's killing him!" "Already has him on the ground." "There's so much blood..."

Not one of the mob members stepped in to put a stop to it. Not one soul in the lot, and they would all feel guilty about it later but by then it would be too late.

One of the kids who ran from the fight went inside and got an adult to come out and see the hell that had been unleashed. Shortly thereafter, a team of guardians and teachers came pouring out of the orphanage building. They were led by the Vice Principle of the school program, Eric Carter. Perhaps the only one to ever take an interest in the boy giant, to spend hours after school, to share books and the occasional soft drink with the impossible loner—he stormed over to where the towering behemoth lorded over the pulpy waste of a body he'd just made quick work of and gently eased his protégé from off of the heap of a boy, now laying in his own blood.

"We've talked about this my son," Carter said,

attempting to sooth away the fires still roaring wildly inside of the boy. "I can't have you reacting this way every time someone calls you a name."

It took the boy several moments to release himself from the bonds of rage for long enough to look up at his mentor, confidant, and perhaps his only friend in the world up to this point. A smile creeped back along the curve of his lips, and he winked and said, "I could see red within myself, even as I watched the red trickle down from his face."

Eric Carter just looked up at the sky, silently asking God for some direction on this one. "Why are you testing me so hard on this?" He asked his Maker, running through half the Catholic catechism in his head. "Your ways are mysterious, but all I'm asking for is one puzzle piece at a time."

But the skies clouded over as if to answer God's servant by shutting him out from the heavens. Soon enough it would rain over the orphanage and the fields; the blood on the ground will soon be washed away, leaving not one trace of the anger and the hate that had been built out among the frustrated souls today.

What may come tomorrow is anybody's guess.

CH. 1: A MAN NEEDS TO GET OUT

Present day, outside of some warehouse in Richmond...

"This is the life we chose," said Johnny Gunn, looking up at the big head blocking his view of the sky beside the side door opening into the warehouse building that served as their boss' base of operations. "You have no reason to break from it now. If you do break you may find yourself being broken. You know that better than anyone Michael Liebowitz."

The big head squinted its eyes as it looked down at Johnny. The head's owner would never let anyone other than Johnny call him by his full given name; everybody else knows him as simply Big Mike. At 6' 10" and a skeleton of the densest bone known to man carrying over 300 pounds of mountainous muscle, to call Mike Liebowitz big was something of an understatement. He tried to take in his close friend's words, though given the years of blunt trauma to the head brought with it a comprehension rate that was rather inhibited as well as a lowered ability to appreciate the gravity of the situation he was putting himself into with retiring from the life. Everything else about the man was still fully capable.

"Are you even listening to me you lout?" Johnny shouted, tapping into Big Mike's shoulder with the business end of his fist. His friend being so much taller than him, he had to rise up on the balls of his feet in order to reach his shoulder. "I see the wheels turning in your head through your glassy eyeballs. Seriously man, when's the last time you got your head examined?" The tone in Johnny's voice was a perfectly blended mix of frustration and concern, with one emotion promptly feeding into the other and vice versa.

Mike shook himself out of his daze and looked down at Johnny, as though really seeing him for the first time. "I'm sorry man. I must've let my mind wander around somewhere." Johnny gave him the same old familiar look he had always given him, suggesting without words that his gargantuan-sized friend might be losing it. "Look," Mike added, "I know it sounds bad to wanna get out now. I'm in my thirties and I'm still young enough to get out and enjoy my life without much of a problem hanging over my head."

"Well that's ok I guess," Johnny interjected, tapping his friend again in the shoulder. "At least you're thinking semi-straight. Now forget this crap for now and let's get inside and report to the boss. It's getting cold out here, and I left my good jacket at home." And with that Johnny opened the side door and walked inside, not even giving Mike a chance to explain himself any further.

Mike paused at the door, allowing for it to slam back into his face. To go in and act like nothing was going on wasn't in the cards for him; but on the other hand the thought of leaving Johnny behind and risking the chance that the boss wouldn't care for his terms of resignation weighed just as heavily on his mind. He couldn't help but to take a few moments to consider the issue at hand, and the issue at hand was beginning to talk back at him with harsh words.

The truth was, Big Mike had been strongly considering quitting his current vocation as enforcer for a good 10 months now. Ever since the last major job went a little off, making it difficult for the boss to bring in that foreign car shipment from Europe and hop and chop them for illegal street racing, Mike started to allow certain doubts to creep in, doubts concerning his line of work. The way he blew up on the guys who were bringing the cargo ship through the port didn't exactly help to fix the problem when it came time to negotiate things further, and ever since then he had felt a lingering hindrance to his relationship with his boss, a man by the name of Robert Christopher. That kind of emotional strife doesn't exactly breed inner confidence, and Mike knew well enough to want to break away while he still felt like he had the chance.

Without very much wanting to, Big Mike groaned once as he opened the door, and then groaned a second time as he tried to squeeze himself through the doorway. *I should've gotten a contractor to put in a bigger one when I had the chance to offer my opinion*, Mike thought to himself. *But if I do end up walking away the added expense would have all been for nothing. And then there the company will be, stuck with another useless expense that did nothing for long term growth.*

Johnny had already gone on ahead of him by the time Big Mike made it into the main hull of the warehouse. Mike took his sweet time walking across the floor, so that by the time he turned the knob on the leading into Robert's office he could hear a voice from inside say, "Big Mike, how nice of you to join us. Please, come in."

Mike swung the door wide open and had to hunch down to get himself through the threshold. He then straightened back up to find the man in charge, Robert Christopher, staring straight at him with his piercing steel eyes. Three of his other enforcers were standing around in his office, eyeing back at Mike. Even Johnny Gunn, making a beeline from his spot in the center of the room in order to stand next to his friend, was looking at him uneasily. The cumulative effect was that of your rudimentary, ordinary

7

staring contest—one where the odds were five against one.

Big Mike did not like those odds, but this time around he figured he'd play it cool. It was his chance at turning in for the gold watch, after all.

"You can take a seat if you wish," Robert said, gesturing Mike to the chair on the guest side of his desk. He and everyone else in the room were standing around, looking content enough to remain standing for a few decades or more. "I caught wind of maybe you wanting to leave from under my employ. I would surely like to try and convince you out of it, if I can."

"You heard right," Big Mike said, eyeing Johnny a moment. "Though this has been a recent development on my part and I'm not sure how it got to you so fast." He shook his head when Robert again offered him the seat. "I needn't take up much of anyone's time on this. Just a quick in-and-out; it's the way you always like your business handled."

"Ah, how I appreciate that sentiment," Robert said, reaching for a bottle of scotch from the cabinet behind him. "Spoken like a real man. All the more reason for me to want you to stay."

"I told him Mister Christopher," Johnny said, so fast that his voice squeaked a bit at the end of every syllable. "I told him you wouldn't want for a man of his caliber to break off—not when so much is on the line over the next few months."

"Shut up," Mike muttered under his breath.

"Yeah Johnny, shut up," Robert said, giving Johnny a cursory glance. He looked back at Mike, opening the new bottle and snapping to the guy to his right. "Get us a couple of glasses would you?"

"I don't drink scotch no more boss," Mike said, putting out a hand. "I stick to cheap beer now. Thank you much though."

Robert frowned and lowered his shoulders, acting very

much like a pouting child. "That's right, I forgot. You don't care for how bad the strong stuff messes with your head. Tell me, does it still hurt between your eyes?"

"Every night before I go to sleep, and every day before it rains," Mike said. He pulled an envelope from out of his pocket and placed it on the desk. "I wrote out some old contacts I have from the years before I joined with you. These cats have some of the same skills as I do, the same military background and everything. I didn't want to leave you hanging before I hung up the coat and all that."

Robert picked up the envelope and held it tenderly with one hand. He gave Mike a meaningful glance, though what the meaning of it could be was anybody's guess.

Everybody just stood around for the next little while, with everyone but the boss feeling evermore awkward with every passing moment. Mike and Johnny could both feel the itch to back their way towards the door and hightail it out of there, but respect and honor prohibited them from scratching that itch just yet. So they just stood there and basked in the awkwardness some more, not quite enjoying the silence but knowing no other alternative than to deal with the hand they were dealt.

Finally, Robert cleared his throat. "I take it you'll be seeing the shrink you been telling me about. Need to talk about the stress induced while on that job a few months back?"

Mike nodded. "I won't get into the details of the job once I see the shrink boss. I can promise you on my life on that. I got some baggage I want to unload at the gate, and the sooner I unload it the better I'll feel. I can get a job driving pallets somewhere and just take it easy a while. Maybe even catch up on some of my reading if I want."

"Yes, your reading." Robert sat the scotch down on his desk and reached down for one of the lower drawers. He opened it and pulled out a couple of paperbacks, the kind one used to could get from the drugstore spinner rack for less than a dollar apiece. He tossed them one by one to Mike, who caught them with a child's grace and dexterity. "There's a couple of them Jim Thompson books I was telling you about. Figured you would get a kick out of them."

Mike nodded as he looked over the front covers of the books. "Thank you boss. I do appreciate it. And again I'm sorry for how that job went down. Them imported cars can be a tricky business."

Robert just waved the whole thing off like it was nothing. "Nah Mike, don't worry about it. My contact shouldn't have poked and prodded you like he did. I warned my whole team from overseas about you being the worst of the worst when it came to temper and destruction. It was on them to have paid attention to what I told them."

"It was the biggest scrape I've ever had to get myself out of," Mike said coolly, shaking his head. "I thank God that I had Johnny guarding my back—I could've sustained more damage to my head than I did, and I wouldn't be standing here talking to you about it."

"From what some of our guys from oversees tell me you did a good enough job on your own, Johnny on your back or no. Even with boxes of tires falling on you, you managed to lay out over three dozen men, and that ain't no joke. One of the reasons I give you a little more room than I do most of my men. Even as you leave from me my son."

Mike grimaced at being referred to as 'son'. Near as he could tell he had no family, so the reference of familiarity felt a tad off.

And so with everything seemingly out of the way Robert around the desk and stood in front of Mike. At sixty years of age Robert Christopher still had the youthful vigor and athletic prowess of a man half his age. He stood almost a foot under Mike's height, but he carried the genes that granted him broad shoulders and good musculature to stand a cutting figure in his own right. He gave Mike a wistful, fatherly look as he reached out with his hand for

Mike to shake. "We'll forego all the formalities and just leave things open ended for you Mike. You want to come on back we'll be glad to have you back. How does that sound to you?"

"It sounds great Mister Christopher. Thank you." Mike smiled down on his (now former) boss as he took his hand and shook it.

Johnny Gunn was shaking and reddening in the face so bad that he was about ready to pop. "Um boss, I don't think we should just let my good partner walk away without extending some kind of package to entice him to stay—"

"I told you to cool it Gunn," Robert snapped, eyeing Johnny with glassy-cold eyes. Johnny caught his meaning and slinked back. Ordinarily a feisty, ornery mess of a man, Johnny knew better than to push his employer too far after being given the last warning.

With everything in good order for the time being Mike told everyone goodbye and tipped them a quick salute on his way out. This time the walk through the main hull of the warehouse was a bit quicker, for Big Mike had a weight lifted off of his shoulders and could relax for a bit.

The chilly night air landed against Big Mike Liebowitz' face as he came out of the building. He stood on the sidewalk for a few moments and raised his face up towards the sky, closing his eyes and breathing in the scents of the city. The nights seem to be the best times in Richmond proper, for it is only at night when the hustle and bustle, noise and silence, highs and lows and everything in between come together and make some kind of sense. After years getting over the backyard of the orphanage, the time spent in Middle Eastern deserts fighting invisible enemies, and now with the illicit career he's built up as a mere underling, Big Mike could feel the sense of calm come over him the likes of which he'd never had before and may never have again.

Mike took a step off of the pavement and made for

where he parked his truck along the adjacent street, stopping in the middle of the street upon hearing his partner yell out after him. "Wait Michael, wait! Hold up a minute will ya?" Mike turned just as Johnny came running up to him, excited as a school child getting out for summer break. "Before you go anywhere, lemme talk with you for a bit."

"How long's a bit Johnny? Cause I'd like to hit up a Waffle House and get a burger before I go home and hit the bed. Been a rough couple of weeks with next to no sleep."

"Well get used to having more of me around than you can stand Mike," Johnny said, slapping his buddy on the back. "Because I managed to wrestle a month's vacation from out of the boss just now." Johnny giggled, alarming Mike. He'd never heard Johnny giggle before, not even once.

"Now why would you go and do a thing like that?" Mike asked, taking his meaty fingers and rubbing the bridge of his nose. "The boss already took a dive by letting me off the hook. I'm sure he wouldn't just up and stand for allowing another hit guy to take off for a month."

"That's the thing though Mike," Johnny said. "You and I have been working together for such a while that he's gonna need some time to think of who to pull up through the ranks and pair with me. That will take some time, leaving me and you some weeks to get into some shifty stuff."

"No, not gonna happen." Mike started for the truck. "I made a break from working for the Syndicate so that I could turn straight for a little while. I'm not down for pulling con jobs, not even if they're with my best friend in the whole wide world."

"It's both flattering and sad that I'm your best friend," Johnny said, following close behind Mike's trail. "In any case, you're not gonna nab just any old job like talking about it. You're currently without a steady ream of funds, and you're gonna need to pad your pocket for a little bit.

I've got a few quick jobs we can do in the meantime. Now just let me bend your ear for a bit."

Mike had no choice but to listen as Johnny bent his ear and rattled off some half-backed schemes for jobs that were three, four, and twenty steps behind what either of them had the talent and experience for. The more he listened, the more than Big Mike Liebowitz could feel the burning in his gut—the burning that never quite left from him, but only lessened and enflamed depending on whether the man was listening to some maddening bull crap. And this was a night for some Supreme A-Level Bull Crap.

Meanwhile back at the office Robert Christopher of the Christopher Crime Syndicate started making some calls. While putting on a friendly face before one of his best enforcers (the problem with the imported cars a few months back notwithstanding), secretly the head boss was furious with the possibility that someone would defect in an effort to seek a straight life. While keeping to the letter of the promise given to every warm body under his employ, Robert figured on pulling some stops in an effort to insure himself against potential issues should they arise.

He dialed a few numbers into his cell and took it to his ear. After several rings a voice picked up and answered. "Time to keep some eyes out on Mike and his partner Gunn," Robert said. He stopped and listened to the voice ask some questions. "No, it's not serious yet. The big guy decided to call it quits, and the little fireplug took some time off to chill with him for a bit." Some more questions from the other end, and then finally. "If push comes to shove it will be a matter of bringing a blast or two from Mike's past out into the light. Let's only hope it doesn't come to that. You have your standing orders, now make it happen you got it?"

And with that Robert Christopher hung up, tossing the phone down on his desk and grabbing the scotch. It was time for a strong drink to settle the nerves and cool him off for a few hours. It was getting late into the night, and the morning was quickly approaching.

CH. 2: IT'S THE SAME OLD STORY

"I don't want to start knocking over convenience stores and diners," Big Mike said, trying his best to get comfortable in the driver seat of his truck. As big as the three-quarter ton diesel was, it was still a pain to fit himself inside the cab. This, coupled with the aggravating conversation thrust upon him by his (now former) partner, brought on the ghostly beginnings of a possible migraine, the likes of which would only serve to annoy the mountain of a man and make him yearn to go back in time to the orphanage and kick the snot out of that pea-brain devil Elmore Johnson once more for good measure.

"You don't wanna do anything," Johnny complained, allowing the soft hint of a pout to enter across his lips. "How many times am I gonna have to push it down your throat kid? You don't know any other life. You've nowhere to go home to, and no other skills or training. Might as well put the skills you do have to use and make some quick cash before you turn around and go to flipping burgers and directing idiots to remodeling and home repair kits for your bread and butter."

Mike started up the truck and let her set in idle while he considered Johnny's words. His hand reached for the radio knobs without anything to go on other than instinct;

Johnny was made to suffer yet again as his comrade flipped it over to an old country station. "Oh now, come on," Johnny cried, "don't make me listen to this crap. You always make me listen to it."

"My truck. My rules." Big Mike didn't say these words so much as he grunted them out, letting them escape from his mouth in much the same way a toad lets out its low-base roar. He shifted the automatic transmission into drive and rolled out of the parking space, creeping along the side street in a crawl so slow a tadpole wouldn't have any trouble keeping up. "Now you know that for an enforcer to lower himself to petty theft is a crime against the fraternity. What would Mister Christopher think if I leave from under him and do low-paying con jobs on my own?"

Johnny guffawed like Mike just told the funniest joke. "What's he gonna say about anything, now that you're self-employed? You know, come to think of it I think you might've made a good decision in cutting ties. Maybe I'll just make my vacation a permanent thing—that is, if you go about this right and do what I tell you."

Johnny leaned back in his seat and started to stretch his legs, content with his own logic and how he was talking about things. Mike gave him the occasional slant-eye as he drove, attempting to process this rapid change in attitude his partner was now exhibiting.

For the next several minutes the two men rode down the bustling city streets in silence, with only the sounds of old country hits coming out of the radio to fill the void built up inside the cabin. It was getting late in the night, bordering on close to two-thirty in the morning, and the night life was in full swing out in the open Richmond air. Every so often Mike would glance out the driver side window, eyeing the working girls as they pick up their johns and the young people who like to dance about like drunken angels while they wait to get into the dancing clubs (with a new place opening up every other week). The light reflecting off of the full moon cast down upon the earth, shining its truth on all the sinners and the lonely ones who come milling about, looking to hide their secrets and knowing that they will eventually be exposed for the imposters they've always been.

After a while the peaceful serenity cultivated within the truck cab was brought down to ruin when Johnny pulled a pack of cigarettes from out of his front pocket and ruffled through it for a smoke. "You don't mind that I smoke in here do ya? I know it's a new truck, but it's really a used one and only new to you so I—"

"Roll down the window and hang it off outside," Mike said, groaning along to the sounds of the old country station. "You know the drill. Same rules, different wheels. Ain't a thing gonna change, except that the world changes all on its own and we have to live under it."

"You're a real pessimist," Johnny snorted, going for the light up with one hand holding the lighter and rolling down the window with the other. "I swear Mike," he added, and then he stopped to get the smoke to catch. He got the light going, took a drag and let the fresh ash out the window. Thus refreshed by the smoke, he turned back to Mike and said, "I swear, you'd of thought that you would be happy as a clam to cut out from the life and working for your own."

"Not really cutting from the life if we're going to knock off a couple places and steal their chump change," Mike said, turning off on a ramp heading onto the highway. "I still wanna find me a steady job, something honest. I could get my forklift license and make good money moving pallets four or five days a week."

"Moving pallets ain't nothing," Johnny said, snapping to life. He started to jump around in his seat like a child waiting to break into some presents on Christmas Day. "A man of your experience ought to go balls to the wall and do his own small-scale syndicate. We could set up our own thing with no problem at all. We would be a two-man syndicate, build ourselves up and end up with more money than we ever did and ever will working for Robert Christopher."

"Look at you changing colors," Mike said, gasping. "When I was telling Mister Christopher that I quit you were practically worshipping at his alter. Now you're just itching to go into competition with him. What's the boss-man going to think about that I wonder?"

"He's not gonna think anything of it" Johnny whined. He was quickly dragging the smoke to near the end where the butt was, and had another smoke in hand for when he finished with the first. "The man's base of operations is in the heart of Richmond; the way I figure it we can hit up some spots in Chase City, South Boston, as well as Buckingham and Cumberland. Any of those spots would be just small enough not to piss the boss-man off, or even to draw his interest."

"Everything draws his interest," Mike muttered, snorting. "Mister Christopher has his hooks in every-which way. You can't do much without him catching on."

Mike reached for the knob and changed the station over to a contemporary religious station, filled with modern Christian music and old-time revival style preaching coming in from Southern Evangelists who haven't made the transition from radio into tv just yet.

"Oh now great," Johnny groaned, throwing out the finished butt and quickly lighting up his next smoke. "We go from hillbilly music to church lady fear-mongering. There ain't no happy medium with you anymore. I wish you would go back to only playing classic rock, or blues, or something with some *life* in it man. You were more fun when you played that stuff."

"Whatever. I'm starting to like this station. It's growing on me a little. And besides classic rock gets a bit too rowdy and violent sounding after a while."

"Uh huh," Johnny said, picking up on of the Jim

Thompson paperbacks from the seat beside him. "Too rowdy and violent sounding. And how many of this guy's books have you read so far? I know you read *The Killer Inside Me*. After 40 or 50 pages even I got a little down on that stuff."

"I'm about to pull into the Waffle House parking lot. You're not going to disrupt my whole breakfast with this kind of talk are you? Because I can drop you off somewhere if you are itching to get booted from out of my truck."

Johnny looked at his watch. "Shoot, it's three in the morning almost. How can you eat a burger this late? Oh wait, excuse me—how can you eat half a dozen burgers this late? That is the more appropriate question to ask considering who I'm dealing with."

"Shut up Johnny. Sometimes you talk too much, and as much as I like you that flaw of yours can get on a man's nerves." Mike pulled into the parking spot and eased the truck into a spot off to the outer side of the restaurant. He then grabbed the book from Johnny's hands and took it with him as he turned off the engine, took out the key, opened the door and climbed out of the truck. The entire vehicle rattled violently back and forth as the elephantine bulk moved from inside the cab to the outside. The hull rattled again as the tree stump of a hand closed the driver door shut.

Johnny sat in the passenger seat for a moment, too stunned to speak, before he got the nerve to hang his head from out of his window and shouted, "You could've been a lot more gentle if you had wanted to!" And with that bit of frustration now off his chest, Johnny got out from the truck and closed the passenger door, making quick work of catching up to his friend.

Mike went for the back spot touching the back end of where the kitchen was placed. He had enough trouble getting into a chair in most restaurants, and he didn't feel much like suffering through a booth this morning. He sat down, nodded toward his usual waitress Brenda, and asked for his usual drink—coffee, plenty of it, black as night and with a snort of Coca-Cola from the fountain. Once he received his precious beverage he cracked open his book and began to skim through the first few pages, taking in a phrase here and a paragraph there, scrutinizing the narrative just enough to determine if the book looked good enough to truly sink one's teeth into.

The truth was that Mike had already read this one, having checked it out from the library. But there was a chance it might still hold secrets for him to uncover, so Mike wallowed in willingly, waiting to see what he might find.

Johnny took a seat next to Mike and called after Brenda. "You all still don't serve beer in here do you? I should have known this was a no-class joint. Only come here because the lug I brought with me can't stand but to come in here every morning around this time."

"You can hush up right now Mister Gunn," Brenda sassed back, bringing over a glass of sweet tea and a straw. She placed these in front of Johnny and gave him a look. "Bryan will be having your usual up in just a few minutes. Try and behave yourselves while he cooks everything for you." She and Johnny shared a knowing laugh, and then she went back to serving the only other table in the place that was currently occupied, filled to capacity with what looked like a quintet of punk-influenced teenagers.

Johnny looked over at Mike and nudged him on the shoulder. "If you would put the book down for a moment and come back to earth I might can have a conversation with you. You wanna read some nonsense go to night school."

Mike groaned as he closed the book and set it off to the side, looking at Johnny thoughtfully. "I do not want to go into the country and knock over gas stations and liquor stores. That's just stupid. If I wanted to still live the criminal life I could have just stayed on Mister Christopher's payroll. The pay's better, and at least with the Syndicate I can anticipate what kind of danger I'd be getting myself into. With some of the hicks running these stations there's no telling who's packing what—one of them could have a bazooka for all I know."

"Now look who's being stupid," Johnny said. "And anyway you don't need to be bringing this up in front of civilians, especially about the Syndicate. Don't want it to get back to the boss that we let on about any of his business.

"The boss—my ex-boss—has a good way of handling his business. I've done my part to honor secrecy, and I don't need you or anyone giving me lip about letting the drop on anything."

"Besides," Mike added, "you were the one who brought it up in here. That was your fault."

"You still like to play it loose every now and again," Johnny said, shaking his head. "I still can't believe you didn't get in any trouble over the maniac stunt you pulled with the imported cars. Could've gotten everyone killed, instead of the dozen federal agents you clipped. And a few thugs."

"And that will be the last I wanna here about the imported car incident," Mike said curtly. He drained his mug and called out for Brenda to refill his drink. After she topped him off he turned back to Johnny and added, "Now I've got some serious thinking to do about how I'm going to earn some honest-to-God money in the next few weeks. And I don't mean of the gas station or liquor store variety either; that's out of the question."

"Why are you so dead set against doing this?" Johnny asked, the whine in his voice growing with every passing syllable. "Remember when we used to pull these little cons back in the early days? When we had too many weeks and months between major jobs and needed to keep ourselves

21

limber and our talents sharp? It will be just like that—just like the good old days when all was good and new and without blemish."

"You're beginning to scare me," Mike muttered.

"Do you want to know what scares me?" Johnny asked. He started to beat into his chest, matching the tempo of every other syllable. "What scares me is to see a beast—a natural born, unpredictable, relentless beast like you—want to turn his back on the life completely and play at Mister Nice Guy. That's something I just don't understand. And unless you are willing to go on one last little run with me, I'm gonna start to feel like this whole time has been a waste between us."

Mike's eyes widened as the food came out to them. "Ah, so that's what this has all been about. It's not about the jobs at all. You just want to end our partnership on a good note."

"I think I'm at least entitled to that."

At this Big Mike couldn't help but to smile, and he could feel a familiar tick in his throat. "Ok then. Why didn't you say so? Sure, I'll do a couple of jobs with you. But I'm going to tell you now, that I do not want any trouble with the boss or the law. We're gonna do the quick in-and-out every time, purely by the book. Do you understand what I'm saying?"

"Yeah, I understand," Johnny said, digging his fork into his chili omelette. "Everything will be as it was when we first went out, back in the good old days."

"Hopefully better than the good old days," Mike corrected.

"Oh Michael, nothing's better than the good old days."

"Whatever you say man. Now let's eat. I'm starving here."

CH. 3: AN OLD FACE COMES TO THE SURFACE

Elmore Johnson, aged 34, carrying a sizable gut around and humped in the back thanks to a herniated disk in the spine. Elmore Johnson, who works as a custodian at St. Francis Hospital and barely surviving under the week-to-week rent at the Extended Stay InTown Suites. Elmore Johnson, who once held an unspoken claim as infantine leader in the orphanage where he once called home—until that fateful day when the monster dealt him a savage beating and took away his power.

Elmore Johnson, hoping for the chance to enact revenge on the one who set his life on the course that led him into the twist-and-turn hell that everything would eventually become, miserable in the here and now. The one whose name is Michael Liebowitz—the boy giant, the freak of nature.

After aging out at the orphanage Elmore managed to work his way through tech school, studying everything he could about software, computers and the practical uses for all things that can benefit one looking to hack into any system anywhere. Four years in the Army, followed by four years in the reserve, Elmore's military career came to a halt when problems arose concerning a petty officer of the female persuasion. How he scraped out of that one without a dishonorable discharge he couldn't guess, until last year, when a man named Robert Christopher walked out from the hospital and ran into Elmore as he was coming off a late shift. "Here's my business card Mister Johnson," Robert said, handing his card over with one hand and shaking Elmore's hand with the other. "I can give you a little side business to supplement your income here. I take great interest in your tech savvy, and could use a man like you. Glad to finally meet the man I was able to help out of a jam."

And thus was given unto Elmore a small glimmer of hope. Something was going to turn up. Elmore could smile again, and finally learn to make the best of a bad situation.

Now coming home to a single room spot, smelling like bleach and sanitizing fluid, removing his outer layers at the door and taking off his work shoes on the way to the kitchenette, Elmore spent the entire shift at the hospital longing for a fresh six-pack of beer to cool his blood from a bubbling broil. A mind wasting as it withdraws into itself, a body that grows sicker with every passing year, the over-grown man child wanted just to fall drunkenly to sleep before the morning rays of sunlight entered into the room through the cracks around the door and ruined the atmosphere that a half-deranged mind had spent so long trying to cultivate.

Stopping in front of the fridge, opening the door and reaching in for that fresh six-pack of alcoholic bliss, and growing cheerful at the fact that each aluminum cylinder was as equally chilled as the next. This wasn't going to be a great night, nor was it going to be a good night; but with enough cold beer to calm the nerves it was going to be an adequate night. Perfectly adequate for a body and soul that's ready to die.

Elmore Johnson was ready to die that day when the boy giant left his own childhood body a bloodied mess on the field in front of his hoard of merry men. His pride and power stripped from him, Elmore decided thereafter to never again let the germ of life enter into his soul. Instead the gates of hell were to remain open to him, only to close after a chance at revenge and redemption can again put a smile on the deposed Orphan King's face.

It was at that moment, just when the Orphan King held the fresh six-pack in his hands (sullied from work that no man of royal blood should have to do), that the phone by the bed began to ring.

Cursing himself for the precious time not spent drinking—and for just now realizing that he'd gone to work without bringing his cell with him—Elmore set the beer on the counter and walked over to the phone. Grabbing the molded plastic mess from its charger, he stood there and cradled the thing in his hand for a moment before answering it. The number on the Caller ID seemed vaguely familiar, but the fogs of memory inside Elmore's head would not allow him to recollect from where he knew the digits. Not wanting to risk it going to voicemail, Elmore decided just to answer it and see what would happen.

"Elmore Johnson's phone," he grunted into the phone. "This is Elmore speaking. Waddya want? I had something I was looking to get into here"

"I told you to commit my number to memory," a familiar voice told him on the other end. "Is this how you talk to a man who gets you out of trouble over every indiscretion concerning women at strip clubs and their bouncer friends?"

"Mister Christopher, how are you?" Elmore's tone changed from demanding and impatient to groveling and pitiful in the span of a second. "I am so sorry—I guess I wasn't paying attention. Been meaning to thank you for the last job you gave me; I'm now starting to build up a semblance of a retirement fund, with a few bucks left over."

"Be sure to talk with the accountant I referred you to," Robert said, "and get him to put some of that money in the stock market. If you want to keep yourself going till you reach the twilight years, the stocks are a man's best bet."

"I will definitely do that Mister Christopher," Elmore said. "Now what can I do for you? Is it something that I need to do right away? Because I did just get home from work, and I was hoping to unwind just a bit; my hernia is acting up more than usual."

"Oh yes, definitely. Do get some rest. I only called you to let you know of one of my former employees who you might be interested in looking after. Mind if I give you his name?

"Sure, lemme just get a pen and paper." Elmore cradled the phone between his neck and ear as he grabbed a click pen and a steno book from the coffee table. Flipping the book to a clean page, he clicked the pen open and said into the phone, "All right. I'm ready when you are."

"Yes well, you may be surprised to know that the name of this former employee of mine is Michael Liebowitz." He cleared his throat and added, "That name ring any bells with you?"

Elmore Johnson nearly dropped the phone from between his shoulder and his ear. He hadn't heard that name spoke in 14 years, not since that day in the back yard of the orphanage when all of a young child's power had been lost in blood. No, that name hasn't been said aloud around Elmore Johnson, though he's surely thought about it constantly over the last several years. The name still sends shivers of fear mixed with rage down Elmore's screwed up spine.

"I don't think I need to write that name down Mister Christopher," Elmore muttered into the phone. He tossed the pen and notebook back onto the table and walked back over to the bed, where he sat down and seemed to deflate into himself. "Is there anything in particular that you would want for me to do in regards to this guy?"

"Oh, it's nothing much my friend," said Robert. "I

already spoke with another man in my employ who has more of a vested interest in handling some affairs concerning this man. I just figured that you could maybe keep a little surveillance on this guy. Maybe hack into his online habits or phone records. Ordinarily I wouldn't waste your time and talents on a former employee, but considering that this one was so near and dear to me I would like to keep some tabs on an old investment. Is there any other information you will need for this?"

"Oh no Mister Christopher. That won't be necessary. I don't need anything else. I'll get on this after some much needed sleep; does that sound good?"

"It sounds good," Robert said, laughing. "All right then. Get some rest and take care. I'll wire you some money to keep you going for a while longer. And remember what I told you about my accountant—just a little in stocks, and even a few bonds, will go a long way along the line."

And with that the man who had done so much to help a guy down on his luck hung up, leaving Elmore to consider this business of fate handing him a golden opportunity.

Michael Liebowitz, the freak of nature. The one who drew first blood and wrecked so much of a man's consciousness and mental stability. The one who possessed him like a demon and left him screaming awake after so many bad dreams. The one who had now left his boss' employ and was now needing to be spied on for a bit. Which left Elmore with the gentle seeds of a plan, not yet developed beyond a few shadowy strings of thought but beginning to stew together into something great. Elmore was going to enjoy getting into this job.

But first, a man was parched. Elmore wanted to drink his six-pack of beer before bed. A few hours of drunken sleep and he can go about developing his plans.

Elmore went over to the counter and grabbed up the beer. They lost a touch of their coldness but were still icy enough to be enjoyed. Elmore decided to take one of the chairs from beside his small dining table and sit outside of his door for a while and drink the beer; he had a bag of cans set for taking down to the recycling place for some cash, and he wanted to add to his haul. He was beginning to wonder if any ladies of the night were going to be doing their walk of shame this early in the morning; if he could play his cards right, maybe one of them might offer him a chance at adding to their shame. After all, a man does have his needs.

Elmore drug one of the chairs out into the early morning air and propped it against the segment of wall that stood between the window and the doorframe. Then he set the six-pack down on the cold cement beside the chair and went back inside to find his dip and a cup to spit in. Besides the ever-growing dependence on alcohol, a man also felt the lingering draw to take on the cancerous gnaw of the tobacco leaves, ground together into precious strips on which to chew and create the familiar tar-ridden juices within the mouth. Dip tobacco, the chewing of flesh—an act of bearing down on the meat and drawing out the essence that had been housed inside. The sweet new addiction, combined with that other sweet known as alcohol, held a man transfixed. And Elmore Johnson had no problem with being held transfixed; he had rested inside of that place before, and had to where he relished in it.

Armed now with his dip and cup, Elmore went back outside and closed the door to half an inch from catching and eased into his chair. He grabbed a can from the plastic rings holding the six-pack together and rested it between his knee and elbow; Elmore knew from experience whilst in the army not to mix the beer with the dip, so he set his other stuff off to the side and used his free hand to grab the can from off his leg and quickly popped the tab with the other hand. He then raised the can up in the air and toasted himself, saying, "Respect to the time we spend in waiting. Soon I will have my revenge; even if the good Mister

Christopher were to tell me tomorrow to hold off I will not stop. No, I will not stop, I will not quit until the freak lays down in a pool of his own blood. Until we are even I can burn in this hell of my own design, for my enemy will know about the fire soon enough."

"Knock it off creep," muttered a voice out in the parking lot.

Elmore looked up to see one of the working girls who frequented this spot leaving from her most recent john, walking her merry self out from here because like all the other girls who worked this beat she didn't dare drive to the job. She gave Elmore the slant eye as she moved down the road, from which she may or may not return again.

Elmore Johnson couldn't help but to watch the woman as she became smaller and smaller under the weight of the morning sun and over the mirage of concrete and pavement. Draining his beer in several long sips, he sat hypnotized by the pendulum movements of some overly feminine hips, the likes of which could make the most chaste man question his own resolve.

Elmore was chaste only due to outside elemental forces beyond his control; it certainly wasn't because of any moral choice. He would have to add that to the list of things about which to complain to God—for now he would just have to drink his beer and think over how he'd like to begin the surveillance job that had been given to him.

Any misstep would be a disaster; Elmore Johnson could not afford to suffer yet another misstep. Success was a must, for the sake of one man's whole entire world and need. The king had once been dethroned, but he will take the seat back soon enough.

CH. 4: THINKING IT OVER

Mike dropped Johnny off at his apartment building and drove home in contemplative silence. The litany of jobs that his partner of four years had thrust on him weighted heavy on the top of his gut, and Mike wasn't the kind of guy to make a habit of letting things weigh heavy on his gut for very long. It was bad enough to go into the office and quit the Syndicate—to actually walk in through that warehouse where he and Johnny had stood around and took part in countless illicit things—and tell Robert Christopher that one Michael Liebowitz, otherwise known as "Big Mike," had wanted out of the game in favor of some honest work and a good shrink with whom to discuss his various emotional problems.

But now Johnny was talking nonsense about doing odd jobs of a thieving nature, and to go into that business would mean to break out on the road, never staying at one place more than a little while. That would leave no time to get in the thick of anything with any one shrink; that wouldn't count the time need for seeking out CAT scans or other procedures to see about the head trauma. Which wouldn't make much sense no matter how many ways one repositioned the problem to look at all the different angles. Even without the brain damage he was certain to have,

Mike knew that was an awful lot for one mind to rest and think about for any length of time.

"I don't know what's wrong with him sometimes," Mike concluded out loud in the cab of the truck. "One moment he talks like someone with some sense; the next he's got a wild hair up somewhere, and I dare not go searching for it." Mike giggled at the concept he just laid out onto himself, as he pulled into the driveway in front of his house and climbed out of the truck, grabbing the book he was looking through at the Waffled House before slamming the door shut with a rattling sound of thunder.

"Will you stop slamming doors so early in the morning!" shouted a bodiless masculine voice. Mike had to spin around to catch sight of the small body holding the balding oversized head that had produced it.

Mike's next door neighbor Kevin Harris was standing out in his front lawn next to his newly installed dogwood tree. He glared at Mike with iced-over black eyes. Dressed in a pair of painted-over slippers, a set lint-covered pajama bottoms, and a blue bathrobe three sizes too big that draped over his skin like a truck tarp covering a runt dog, Kevin Harris cut a peculiar picture on this particular morning.

"Why, good morning Kevin," Mike said, waving to his neighbor. "I'm sorry, I didn't see you there. Coming in from the night shift and didn't realize how loud I was being. I'll do my best to keep it down from here on out though. You have my word on that."

"You been telling me that noise every time you come into the neighborhood at this ungodly hour and make a ruckus," Kevin screamed, high pitched as he inched closer to the line dividing Mike's property from his own. "What I want you to tell me is this: I want for you to tell me what kind of job has a man out all night and driving around in a high-dollar diesel truck. That's what I want for you to tell me, and I mean tell me right now!"

"I told you before that I work in security detail," Mike said, shifting his gaze from his neighbor to the precious truck he had setting in the driveway. "Private business, good money. I've put in the work so I can live my vision American dream, and for a large part I attained all of that. My only wish is that you can someday follow in my steps, so that you can fulfill your own dreams." Mike bookended his little spiel with a toothy grin, with his thin lips drawn taught against his gums so as to look rather silly smacked across his clownish face, resting on top of a bovine head. It would be enough to put anyone ill at ease.

Kevin Harris wasn't ill at ease. He was pissed beyond conventional human limits. Crossing both feet over into Michael Liebowitz' property, he jabbed a crooked finger into the big man's chest and said, "I'll have your head man. I want you to know right now that I don't like you. Don't matter to me that half the neighborhood's too scared to confront you about anything. To me you're nothing more than a con man and a freak!"

Ah, but the neighbor-man with a tarp for a bathrobe shouldn't have called Mike a freak. He had no way of knowing, but to do so would mean to court death. In his overblown and unneeded rage, he had taken his own life in his hands; in so doing he would forever alter not only his own health and safety, but also the trajectory of Big Mike Liebowitz' life.

The first thing that Mike did (upon hearing himself being referred to as a "freak") was to grab Kevin by the frayed collar of his bathrobe. He then drew him up from the ground and got him at eye level, leering at him like a diseased hyena looking over a selection of raw meat. He stared at the rattled neighbor-man for several long moments, letting the space between them simmer to a broil from a thousand electric shocks. Then without warning he let of a single bestial roar right in poor Kevin Harris' face, taking his left arm into his hand and twisting it until there was the distinct sound of bones cracking, like the crack of a gun thundering a shot at a close distance from its intended target.

It had become Michael's turn to go angry against his fellow man, and as Kevin Harris was quick to learn the lumbering giant's capacity for rage outclassed his own in every conceivable fashion. He'd been made to behold the presence of a massive, awe-inspiring power, the likes of which couldn't be stopped by anything on this earth.

This was a time for death, this was a time for murder—

"I'm calling the police!" screamed a voice from across the street. Mike turned around to see another neighbor by the name of Mitzi Kelly. An elderly, overweight woman in a nightgown and with hair curlers fitted on the top of her head, she cut a picture nearly as absurd as the whimpering Kevin. She stood there watching the scene unfold, her mouth wide open and her eyes bulging out of her skull. She had her cell phone in hand, flipped open and ready to dial.

"I'm calling the police!" she shouted again, punching the numbers into her phone. "I knew that you were trouble. From the moment you moved into that house I knew! I'll call the police, and I'll have their dogs hunt you into the ground!"

Mike knew then that he screwed up. He'd fallen into the trap, laid out by the rawest of emotion—he'd allowed the rage to get the better of him, and in doing so he unleashed that which had been caged since the incident concerning the import cars. Now he'd exposed himself in front of civilians and risked having the police coming down on him.

I had better get out of here, Mike told himself. *I'd better go now and beat out the police. I cannot risk getting caught!*

He dropped Kevin to the ground, where he rolled around in tears of pain. He ran around to the driver side of the truck and climbed inside, starting the engine And pulling her out of the driveway. Mike didn't even bother to look where he was going—he just drove faster than the hellhounds of the apocalypse, and after making it a few miles down some quiet streets he knew Mike pulled out his phone and dialed Johnny Gunn's number.

"I just saw you Mike," Johnny groaned on the other end. "Why're you calling me and keeping me from getting some sleep? Whaddayawant, whaddayawant, whattayawant?"

"I want you to meet me at the chop-shop pronto," Mike demanded into the phone. "Hurry up and come along—we gotta repaint the truck and change out the plates. Then we had better make a run for a little while, because I can't be seen for at least a few months."

"Oh good god Mike," Johnny complained, "this is getting ridiculous. When we spoke last you were pretty adamant about going straight, and you only begrudgingly accepted my job proposal. Now you want to go into hiding and use stolen plates to get out of...out of...wait a minute, what is it that you got yourself into? You have me stumped now."

"Just meet me at the hangout," Mike snapped, seeing flashing lights up ahead and feeling a touch of dread hit him in the gut. "And please be quick about it."

"Ok Mike geez! I'm coming, chill out..." As he spoke Mike could hear Johnny move around in his apartment; this was then followed by the occasional ruffling of clothes. "I'll be bringing a weekend bag of clothes by the way. Sounds like we'll be taking an extended trip somewhere, and I want to make sure I can change if I need to."

"Just hurry up and get going please," Mike demanded. "See, this is why I keep a weekend bag in the toolbox. For all the smack you talked about preparedness, you always fail on this regard."

"Doesn't sound like a man wanting my help to me," Johnny said. "Tsk-tsk-tsk. Guess I'll just crawl back into bed and catch some sleep. I have my vacation to think about here."

"Come on Johnny, don't leave me in the lurch!" Mike pulled down an underpass and cut through to one of Robert Christopher's chop-shops that also served to disguise vehicles for current and former employees of the Syndicate. "I just pulled up. I'll be waiting for you, but I can't wait long. Now please, hurry up and help a brother out. I'm in a bind!"

"I'm on my way Mike," Johnny answered, and then he hung up.

Mike put his phone back in his pocket and let his truck idle at the big garage-style door till one of the mechanics opened it and motioned for him to come on inside. It wouldn't take much time at all for the guys to give the truck a new coat of paint and some license plates. They would probably replace the wheels and add a hood decal for good measure, if Mike had a mind for any of those things. It was just that Mike wasn't so sure in the heat of the moment how much of a mind he had for anything, considering what had happened.

Why'd I have to do that, Big Mike thought to himself. And then he parked the truck inside the building, walked over to one of the walls, and punched a dent into the concrete.

CH. 5: THE BOSS TAKES HIS SHOT

Robert Christopher was sitting at his desk, listening to the radio and tossing back one glass of scotch after another. It had gotten so that Robert Christopher was always finding a way to keep the drinks forever flowing into him, for to take in more than one social drink among friends and associates was to dishonor one's own reputation, but most certainly in private, during those rare moments when there's not much going on, Robert Christopher gave himself over to the same vice that afflicted over half the men under his employ.

This business of Big Mike quitting the business and seeking a straight job had Robert feeling every kind of bad. Michael Liebowitz was a good enforcer, and had for the most part served the Syndicate well. The only bad mark on the 'screw-off' column for ole Michael was the rampage he went on during the whole imported care debacle—a rampage that put a dozen good men in the hospital with every bone broken in their body, as well as a sharp strain to Robert's international relations. Were it not for Mike's resourceful venture into the drug operation in Powhattan, he would've been taken care of right away. But Mike was a man who recognized his own shortcomings, and he took the needed time to make the necessary reparations to his lord and master.

But now the servant has chosen to break away from the life, and Robert can't help but feel the deep-seated pains of rejection. So he drank his scotch and took a look at himself through the glass. He didn't like what he saw, but it's the best that a man had when he could no longer hold on to the façade he had so carefully crafted, the one that he had presented to his underlings and rivals for so long.

Robert was just about to pour himself another scotch when his phone rang. He sat the glass on his desk and picked up the phone. "Hello?" he grunted into the receiver. "Hurry up whoever you are—I am in no mood to handle business right at this moment."

"Mister Christopher? Of the Syndicate? This is Officer Grubbs. With the Richmond Police Department? I was instructed to contact you over a situation we have here."

Robert quickly changed his tune. "Yes Officer Grubbs. How's the Commissioner doing? Did he throw you guys a steak and beer party like I asked him to?"

"Oh he did Mister Christopher. Thank you for that. Most of the boys loved the new label. Now the reason I called you was to tell you we have a problem concerning the big guy today. Seems he got into a scuffle with his neighbor, broke his arm and dropped him to the ground. Then he drove off, and we've put out an APB on him."

Robert listened to the officer talk with grave intent. When the officer had finished, Robert said, "You were right to come to me with this. While I have no doubt that you could easily find Mike, I would consider it a favor if you'd allow me to handle the matter personally."

"We would have to conduct our own investigation," Officer Grubbs said to him. "Course we would be most glad to work with you in an effort to find Mike. We believe him to have made out with his partner, Johnny Gunn—had a squad car go and check his apartment out, but it was a no-go. The commissioner was hoping to ask for any information you have personally to assist with all this."

"You go ahead and let the commissioner know that I'll be in touch. Thank you for reaching out to me regarding this. Goodbye." And with that Robert hung up the phone, taking his half-drained glass of Scotch into his hand as he reclined back into his chair. Thoughts weighed heavy on his mind as he considered his options for several long moments.

The Richmond Police had every resource available to locate one lone ex-enforcer and his buddy. The fact that Robert had half the force on the Syndicate books ought to have suggested an overlap between dirty uniformed men and some other men who didn't wear uniforms but were no less dirty. But Robert Christopher was smart enough to know not to bridge the two groups of men who worked for him; if the chain of command were kept from connecting it made it harder for some upshot Assistant D.A. to patch them all together and follow them back to him. This proved to work for Mike's advantage, and Robert Christopher was met with a sudden moral dilemma.

Mike was poised to go far off into the deep end, so he needed to be stopped. But even as much as it was necessary, Robert couldn't help but feel for the young man. He snatched him from out of the army, listened to his story of woe concerning a less than ideal upbringing, and bonded more with the deranged giant than he bonded with his first and second wives. This situation was already convoluted as it was, and as Robert reached over and picked the phone back up he knew it was going to get even more convoluted before it was over.

Robert dialed some numbers and put the phone to his ear, listening to the awkward hum of the ringtone. A voice picked up on the other end, and Robert went head-first into his spiel.

"Hey there Sheriff, how are you? Are the streets of Chase City clean and safe? That's good, but listen for a moment. I ought to tell you that I know about your son—you know, the one that you and Brenda gave up at the orphanage, the one you've felt guilty for ever since. I wanted to give you the news, because there might be a chance that you'd get to meet the wayward child soon enough. I just thought you would want to know."

There were some frantic words screeched on the other end, but Robert had said his peace and was done with the matter for now. "I'll give you more information when such information is needed," he said into the phone, and then put the receiver down into the holder. He grabbed the scotch glass back up and took another sip, leaning back into his chair and pondering some disparate thoughts which were in some need of patching together for the good of the future.

The Syndicate was entering into a small world of trouble, and it threatened to implode on itself at any moment. But Robert Christopher was not without some mental resourcefulness, and he knew that things were good.

For now at least. So long as the world doesn't stop in the next several days, things were good. But with the scotch and other fiery liquids quickly running low on supply, Robert couldn't guarantee so much as the next several minutes.

He'd better be careful from here on out.

CH. 6: MIKE & GUNN, INC.

"I don't know what happened back there," Mike said, groaning against the back wall of the shop. He was nursing one can of soda after another, rubbing the top of his aching head with his free hand and rocking back and forth on the balls of his feet. He talked as Johnny stood next to him smoking a cigarette, but he might as well have been talking to a ghost, or nothing at all with the way he was feeling.

"One minute I was having a nice talk with a not-so-nice man," Mike continued, his booming voice wavering just a bit. "Next thing I knew Missus Kelly was calling the law on me after I'd broken my bastard of a next-door neighbor's arm. Now I have to tread lightly until I get out of the city, because I just know that word of this will reach Mister Christopher before long."

"The ole boss-man's the least of your worries," Johnny said, dropping the finished butt to the ground and smooshing it under his boot. "There's a war coming along that you don't even know about, and the cops who aren't on the take will be bringing their big guns."

Mike eyeballed Johnny hard, suddenly forgetting the headache and the bodily pains in favor of breaking down the news he had just been told. "What are you talking about Johnny? What kind of war is coming? What do you know, and for how long have you known? Were you ever planning on telling me about this?"

Johnny smiled weakly, drawing another cigarette from a pack. "Robert Christopher is losing a grip on the company. Cracks are growing all over the Syndicate, and the boss-man's starting to crack under the pressure." When Mike's expression didn't change Johnny continued. "Ever since the import car situation the Syndicate has been taking a hard hit on its reputation with other crime families. People who have been loyal to us are now considering defecting over into other orgs, and the money's still coming in but it's not flowing as heavy now. The only loyal ones that are left are the lesser groups, the runts that nobody wants. Like that Wyatt guy heading up down in Florida."

Then Johnny paused a moment to take the cigarette to his mouth and light it, breathing in that first precious drag of smoke inhalation. After savoring the stilted yellow flavor, he looked back at Mike and said, "Face it kid. You were good while it lasted, but one false move and everything else begins to crumble in your wake." He started to laugh, but the smoke got in the way and he began coughing and hacking, the sounds from his mouth reverberating off of the concrete walls of the shop.

Mike couldn't believe it. "I can't believe it," he said, shaking his head. He walked away from the wall and began to pace the floor for a bit, allowing his feet to eventually lead him over to the vending machine, where he dug out some quarters and plugged them into the slot. He pressed the button for a can of Coke, and as luck would have it two came barreling out instead of one.

"Well hey, at least I can have extra sugar in my bloodstream now," Mike said, but he couldn't bring himself to laugh. All he could manage to do was to drag his feet to where he'd left Johnny and lean against the wall, opening one of the cans and draining it with a few healthy swallows.

"You drink enough of those and you'll get diabetes," Johnny said.

"Smoke enough of those and you'll get lung cancer," Mike said, swallowing. He pointed to the fresh cigarette that Johnny was now pulling from his pack.

"Well hey, it's not like I joined the Syndicate for the health benefits. What do I care anyhow?" Johnny made to laugh again, but the phlegm and the smoke were keeping him from doing a full one.

"You seriously have to quit that habit," Mike complained as he opened his next soda can. The headaches were making the rounds again in full force, but he did his best to ignore them. He would rather have been anywhere other than where he was, doing anything other than what fate had decided for him to do—he chose to ignore this fact as well. A man had to play the cards he'd been dealt, and so long as he had a partner at the poker table he could manage a little more in the long run.

Johnny finally quit hacking for long enough to scowl at his friend. "You seriously have to quit hassling me," he commanded, as he put away the rest of the pack. He had chosen to ignore the cravings for the moment, in favor of salvaging what he had left of his lungs.

Mike and Johnny then stood there in relative silence, casually giving each other their best and angriest looks. In all this time that the two had worked together, there hasn't been so much as a coarse word between them. But between Mike's termination of employment and the subsequent missteps in this other business with the neighbor, there was plenty for one to be course over. In the space of less than 12 hours, two best friends and grown adults were ready to claw at each other's throats like jilted children—only neither one of them was able to come right out and say what it was they were thinking.

To admit to the sudden rage and hate would have been the greater sin.

It was Johnny who decided to break the silence. "So what are your plans for after getting the truck finished up? Even though you agreed to it back at the Waffle House, I know for sure you're not thinking of going with the plans that I laid out. You made your position clear on that, and I know better than to push you when you're set in your own way."

"I ain't as stubborn as everyone makes me out to be," Mike said, dropping the empty can in a nearby bin. He had a moment of thought, and then he walked over and punched another hold into the wall with the added forced of a bestial scream.

"Woah there Mike!" Johnny shouted. "What is wrong with you now?"

"It's nothing. I only just now realized that I must've dropped the book I started reading when I hightailed it away from the dang house. Was really starting to get into it too."

Johnny gave his friend a look. "Are you being serious right now? You punch a hole in the wall—a five-inch thick concrete wall—and get you get all bent of shape and scare the stuffing out of me. And over what, a stupid book? You got some problems to work out man, and I mean work them out *today* mister!"

Mike came up and got into Johnny's face. "You don't get to tell me what to do," he stated flatly, furrowing his brow so that it looked like one big furry caterpillar covering the space over his eyeballs. "I've been working under the beatdown of your words for long enough—it's time that I get to tell you what to do a time or two."

Johnny wasn't having any of his vastly bigger friend's bull; he took a step forward and matched Mike's glare down to the slope of his furrowed brow. "I could turn around now and go back to my apartment. Call up one of my girlfriends and ask them over for a little bit of fun. Enjoy the full term of my vacation and forget all about you. But if you push the

Kid in a corner, and you may just find the Kid grow up on you fast. You won't like what he'll bring with him."

At this Mike tried to keep his composure, standing his ground for a full thirty seconds before bursting out with laughter to fill the walls with enough decibels to shake them down to the foundation. "Oh my god," he said, trying to hold back the tears with a meaty finger, "I cannot believe that you gone back to calling yourself the Kid. Thought you had buried that one long ago."

"Quit laughing at me you ninny," Johnny said, pouting. "That's not fair of you to laugh at me. You came up with your share of crummy names over the years." But even as he said the words he couldn't help but to quickly turn his frown into a wry little smile, and after a few moments he was laughing along with Mike.

All was forgiven faster than it took for a pot of coffee to percolate.

One of the mechanics walked over and handed Mike the keys to his truck. "All right my man, we have her all finished up. The paint's now a nice shade of silver-grey, and the license plates are some of them "Don't Tread On Me" Tea-Party vanities."

Mike gave the mechanic a look. "Tell me you're joking."

"Joking about what, the color or the plates? I'm afraid we did them both. Good news is with all the other detailing we did inside and out you'll be driving nearly a completely different set of wheels. No one will even know it was yours." And with that the mechanic walked off, shaking his head and muttering to himself.

Mike inspected the keys in his hands for a moment before shifting his gaze back at Johnny. "Can you believe that noise about the Tea Party plates. Thought that they died away years ago."

Johnny just shrugged his shoulders. "I try and not get into politics when I can. Too much evil-doing and corruption enter into the mix, and I hold no quarter for such evil things." He paused a moment and then added, "So, what're you planning on doing now? You gonna go into hiding and live off of your precious savings that you got stowed away all over the place?"

Mike shook his head. "Not sure that I can touch my money for the time being. Between Mister Christopher and the remaining fuzz that's not on his payroll I am sure to catch more than a little hell were I to go into any one of the banks to make a withdrawal. I'm gonna have to come up with something right quick though, because I'll need a few dollars for food and lodging while I figure this whole thing out."

"This may be a bad time to bring something up," Johnny said, smirking. "But I'll go for broke and bring it up again anyway. Why don't you let me tag along with you, and we can simply put my little plan to the test? Wouldn't hurt to just try it out and see where it goes. Hit up a handful of stores, make some floating-around money, and keep ourselves in truck-stop steak and beer until we can figure out some big score to work out and Mister Christopher and the fuzz will begin to forget all about us. How about it man, whaddaya say?"

"I say no deal," Mike said, shaking his head. "There's too many risks involved, not the least of which is this sudden and care-free attitude you adopted concerning Mister Christopher. I don't like the constant back and forth you're trying to sell me, and frankly it's putting a touch of doubt into my mind."

"Not a thing about my attitude being sudden," Johnny said. "You just haven't been paying attention to what's going on around you. I've watched everything at it goes down, and here lately the clock's been counting down on Mister Christopher and the Syndicate. I for one don't like how things are going, and I'm smart enough to see about breaking off on my own while I've got the time to do it. And I was hoping that you'd be smart enough to join up with me, seeing as we been friends and partners for so long. But I guess I was wrong about that..."

Johnny started to pout again, playing the odd game that he'd played so often with his bigger riding partner, the one where he pumped up the hurt and the heartache in order to tug at the heartstrings. It was a dirty game to play on a best friend, but you do what you have to do. And besides Mike was guilty of a game or two, every now and again. He could stand to take a little gaming himself, and that's just what he was going to take, in the here and now.

Mike was just about to say something—anything—to pull him out of this awkward predicament in which he found himself. He secretly hated it whenever Johnny put him on the spot, and he wanted very much to express that in no uncertain terms but the terms just seemed to want to escape from his mind at the moment and that too was causing the behemoth some discomfort.

But just when the behemoth was starting to form the words, the distant sound of police sirens pulled him out from his daze and put him right back into the smack-dab of reality. "Oh crud, do you hear that? We've got to get out of here."

"Nah-uh. I ain't going nowhere till you give me an answer Mike."

Mike was already inching toward his newly refurbished truck. "We really have to get out of here Johnny. I don't have time for any more of your shenanigans. We have to leave *now*."

"Tell me we can pull some small con jobs and I'll go with you now."

"Knock it off Johnny. This is no time to be messing around."

"This is no time to be leaving me hanging on a serious question."

"It's not a serious question, and you aren't a serious person. You're not only wasting my time, but you're risking your own life. I don't want that digging into my conscience tonight."

"Fine, so you don't want my life digging into your conscience? Then trust me on my plan and I'll be glad to go along with you. It's really that simple. Come on Big Guy, don't act like you don't want to pull a gang-of-two on some five-and-dime suckers and get away with it big time. I know you well enough to know you love the danger and risk involved in any hair-brained scheme. Mine's just the hairiest of them all; it's really not a big deal. You're just being chicken."

Mike could hear the sirens growing louder, signaling that they were getting nearer. He wanted nothing more than to turn around and jump into the truck, driving off and leaving Johnny and the rest of his former life behind, but a part of him knew that wasn't possible. As much as he wanted something different, this was what Mike had been dealt. And when you're dealt a bad hand you can only play or pass, and to pass was to surrender into death.

There was no way Mike was going to surrender into death, not yet at least. That much had been certain on the outset.

"Ok," Mike said, groaning. "I'll do a couple of small cons with you. I'll be needing the money anyway, and I can't make myself seen at any of the banks just yet." Mike then pointed a finger at Johnny's chest and added, "But I will not be taking any orders from you. We'll be equal partners on this—I'm not going to be your underling for so much as a second. Do you catch my meaning?"

"Geez Mike, chill out," Johnny said, making for the truck. "We've gotta get out of here before the cops bust in and break our heads. And of course we'd be equal partners; how else are we gonna manage an operation like this? Seriously brother, you had better catch your grip back before we both lose ourselves."

And so with that Mike and Johnny each grabbed their

duffle bags from off the ground, each of them filled with enough clothes to last a few days, and climbed into the newly changed truck. Mike waved goodbye to the guys who'd done the work in record time, and then he started the engine and pulled out of the building using the other entrance that led out into an underground road that no one in Richmond City proper knew anything about. Not even the police who were on Robert Christopher's payroll knew anything about this hidden road. By the time the cops pulled into the front of the warehouse Mike and Johnny were gone, not to be seen again for a little while at least.

The looks on every one of the cops' faces upon realizing they'd reached a dead end were so priceless, the mechanics working in the shop wanted to bust out laughing right in their pig faces. Only their fear of being gunned down kept them from making such a grave mistake.

Meanwhile in the truck Mike and Johnny were laying out the particulars to their new partnership. Mike was paying only half attention, keeping the other half to the underground road that he'd only been on a handful of times, the last time being more than six months ago. "We'd better not make too intricate a plan if we do this," he said, feeling the foggy remnants of yet another headache rattle inside him. "If we make things too complicated it could all blow up in our faces."

"Don't worry about it baby," Johnny said laughing, as he pulled out his gun from where he'd hidden it behind his shirt and jacket. "We're Mike and Johnny Incorporated, Master Robbers Extraordinaire. The only plan we need is to walk right up into a place, take out our guns and *bam!*—we blow our enemies in their faces. It's that simple."

Johnny laughed again, and kept on laughing, to the point where Mike had to switch on the radio just to drown the guy out. He was getting anxious, he was feeling the weight sink down into the pit of his stomach, and he very much regretted his decision to go along with this. But it was too late, oh god it was too late.

If one more thing goes wrong the two of them would realize just how late it would be.

CH. 7: ROBERT CHRISTOPHER STARTS IT OFF

Robert Christopher had one of his men drive him to the house where Big Mike made his home. Once he got there he took a quick look around to see exactly what it was he could sniff out this time of day, and was surprised to find one of the Jim Thompson books strewn out on the asphalt of the driveway. He turned to one of the officers now investigating the scene and asked if he could take a look at the book.

"I'm sorry sir," said the officer, shaking his head. "I can't let you move things around on a crime scene. We don't want you contaminating any of the evidence."

"Oh I assure you I won't harm your investigation in any way," Robert said, smiling. He called over Officer Grubbs and shook his hand. "I want to thank you again for letting me know about the situation that happened here today, Officer Grubbs. Would you mind telling your colleague here to allow me to help out in any way that I can?"

Officer Grubbs nodded and turned to his fellow officer. "He has the authority to pretty much do as he please. Better let him do what he asks." He then nodded to Robert and went back to what he was doing, leaving his fellow officer to answer to this new man in charge.

Robert smiled again as he looked upon the young man

in uniform standing before him. "Would you be so kind as to pick that book up and bring it to me? My knees are stiff anymore and I can't bend down like I used to. The problems of growing old." He laughed at his own little bland joke, knowing to the fullest extent just how intimately creepily he was letting on, just by existing.

The young officer went over and picked the book up from off the middle of the driveway and brought it back to Robert, holding the thing away from his body like it was some religious object that was set to obliterate him from the terrestrial realm. He handed it over to Robert; once the thing left his hands he promptly turned and walked off to handle other police business.

The officer, like most other incorruptible souls, knew instantly that he didn't like this strange man. He wanted very much to be done with him as soon as was possible.

Robert Christopher couldn't help but to laugh hysterically at the way he got under the young policeman's skin; it had been so long since he'd managed to toy with one of the newly minted, not yet corrupted spirits donning the badge and holster. He was proud of the talents he'd cultivated over the years, not the least of which was the inane ability to pinpoint the exact members of the Blue Fraternity who have yet to give themselves over to the wrong side of the law, and then to begin chiseling away at their spirit until their indominable wills have been stripped of any and all resolve. It used to be that such tactics were good only because they helped to punish a man mentally until he was willing to join up with the Syndicate and say 'Be Done With It,' but after a while it got to where it was simply too much fun not to engage in a little bit of emotional torture every now and again.

The boss-man considered all this with great humor and interest as he flipped through the book and inspected every other page. He began to wonder about the man who'd possessed it moments before tossing it aside and leaving it at the site of a criminal act of assault against one of his neighbors. Michael Liebowitz was a mystery and always has been—at least he was when he showed up inside of Robert's office looking for a job a few years ago. A mountain of a man with an unpredictable genius inside that melon of a head, Robert knew he would be able to put the young man to good use. It was only when the gentle giant turned out not to be so gentle, when he showed a violent and economically dangerous streak at times of extreme stress and anger, that the head of the Christopher Crime Syndicate had started to wonder if he'd made the right decision in hiring the man.

I thought I could trust you, Robert thought to himself. *I thought I could make an honorary son out of you, like I did with Johnny Gunn. You were to go under his wing, learn the ropes, turn into a fine foot soldier, which you did. But Johnny was to also mold you into something else—into a man, a leader, someone who can make the world into something other than a vehicle for your own twisted pain and revenge...*

The problem with the whole thing was Johnny. He'd never been so great to begin with, had always had his share of failings which served to counteract the good points he did possess. Robert should've known better to have brought him or the mountain of a man onto his team, but Robert Christopher was not a boss who could be accused of not taking risks to test the waters of success. In terms of these men it was becoming a problem of a flash-flood, threatening to destroy the world that one man had spent most of his life trying to build from the ground up.

Robert closed the book and started to look at the cover. It was a Black Lizard paperback edition of *The Killer Inside Me*. Long considered to be Jim Thompson's masterpiece, though not without its pulpy charm. It suddenly occurred to Robert that in many ways Mike was not unlike the sadistic narrator of the book, the deputy sheriff by the name of Lou Ford. In both cases one was left with a man, with a mind which at first appeared to be rather dull and not quite right—amiable to be sure, but not someone you'd want for a high school quiz night. But if you were to look below the surface, truly dug around, you would find not quite a man but an animal: the fierce intelligence of a tiger, with the hooks set to ensnare you if you weren't careful. A man who can hide not only his casually evil brilliance, but also a mind split down the middle, is not a man who can be trusted in the long run.

In the case of Michael Liebowitz Robert had made a big mistake of being all too trusting. Now he was learning to suffer in leisure for the crime he committed in haste.

Holding the book in his hand, Robert Christopher could feel every piece of his interior break apart. This was bigger than the current problem with Michael, and this was a threat realer than the layers of alcohol that a body plastered on itself over and over in the midmorning hours. With every second that passes the risk that had been presented grew bigger, and as head of the Syndicate Robert couldn't allow it to continue a second longer.

It was time for Robert to call in that favor that was owed to him. He needed to phone Elmore and tell him to go ahead and do every and anything that was in his power to do. Money was no option, and neither was secrecy. The only thing a man couldn't afford to lose, was time.

Robert pulled his phone from his pocket and dialed a number. He brought it to his ear and let it ring. After a few moments a voice picked up on the other end and grunted out a rough salutations. "Hello Mister Johnson. I just wanted to go ahead and see about getting to get to work on the Liebowitz case. Things have started to come to a head, and time is of the essence. I'll be most grateful for your services, and am prepared to reward you handsomely."

Elmore was only all too willing to get started, talking excitedly on the other end of the call about what kinds of tracking tech he could implement, as well as the high-clearance satellites that he could hack into and the like. Robert wasn't really interested in any of the mundane details but he listened anyway; he knew better than to make any fuss that could scare off someone who can be of most use to him at any given moment.

"That's all well and good Mister Johnson," Robert said, signaling the end of the conversation. "I'll be glad to hear from you again very soon. Just keep up the good work." And with that he hung up without so much as a goodbye, satisfied that he'd gotten a desperate soul to do his dirty work yet again.

You are a master of men, Robert said to himself. *Even with Mike and Johnny turning their backs on the empire you've built, still there plenty of other dopes on whom you can dump all your anguish and hatred for the civilized world and her good and faithful citizens. After years of suffering from so many hindrances to progress, you will overcome and create that which can never be taken away. No overgrown monstrosity and half-sized loser is going to get in the middle of that.*

Some horrific screeches from across the street pulled Robert away from his pep talk to himself, and when he turned around to see what the fuss was he couldn't quite mask the look of contempt on his face. Upon seeing Mike's neighbor Mitzi Kelly, still dressed in her nightgown and with the hair curlers starting to unravel from out of her head, the look of contempt quickly eroded into mild humor and goodwill toward men.

"Hello ma'am," Robert said loud enough to cut through the screeching. He started walking over to where the woman was with an air of authority in his step. "You wouldn't happen to be the one who called in this horrific incident would you?"

"That's right I called it in," Mitzi shouted. She looked Robert with a determined gaze, sizing him up the way a frequenter of buffets would size up the selection at a new eatery that just opened up in town. "It was unbelievable. To think that I had to bear such a hateful thing. In front of my house no wonder! Just goes to show you that you can never tell who's good and who's bad in this world."

"That's right ma'am," Robert said, smiling. "Some things hide among us, in broad daylight if you can believe it. Better be careful now—no telling who might come creeping along your door."

"Who'd you say you were again?" Mitzi asked, slowly backing away from the man who had come to talk with her. She was clutching to her nightgown so tightly that her knuckles were turning to white.

But Robert didn't answer the fearful neighbor lady, for he was ready to get back into his car and be driven back to the office and the warehouse. He'd gotten as much as he could get from this place, and there was no use sticking around any longer, now that the wheels were in motion.

CH. 8: ELMORE SEARCHES FOR GHOSTS

Elmore Johnson was happy to get to work. More apropos to the feeling in his gut, he was happy to get to work on this one particular task that had been given to him, offered in secret by a boss who understood to the fullest extent what his abilities were. To be recognized in such a way as this was just so amazing that Elmore couldn't help but to jump for joy when he decided to go down to the hospital and hand in his resignation personally.

"I'm pleased to announce that I quit," Elmore said to his boss. He was beaming from ear to ear as he said those words. "I'm now off to bigger and better things. I don't need you or this crummy place!" Then he threw his nametag and set of keys at the man and walked out laughing; he had been set free, and in freedom he no longer had a care in the world.

With the job out of the way Elmore raced drunkenly back to his place, moving his beater of a car all over the road and praying to whoever was listening for the cops to be elsewhere as he sped along the side roads and highway. The cops turned out to be nowhere in sight (thank God, whoever he/she was), and even if somebody did stop him Elmore would only have to mention his current employer's name. More often than not, the words *Robert Christopher* would be enough to put a stop to any and all mischief directed toward an alcoholic taskmaster on his way home.

Elmore liked having the power to shrug that and all other burdens of the world from off his shoulders.

As soon as Elmore made it back to the extended stay and entered the door of his place he went straight for the bed. He bent down as carefully as he could and began to crawl under the bedframe (giving careful consideration to his hernia) , pulling out from underneath a large black military-grade plastic carrying case. He got up from the floor and carried the case over to the dining table, where he gently set down the case and unclasped the fasteners on the sides and raised the top. Then he gingerly began to pull out an oversized laptop, a massive and custom made prize of technology and stealth that served as Elmore's pride and joy over everything else in his miserable excuse of a life.

"Ok then," Elmore said out loud, "time to buckle up and get to work now." He then placed his laptop along the flat surface of the table. This sacred act done with the utmost care, Elmore went ahead and eased down into his chair and opened the computer. He powered her up and typed in three different passwords to log in; once he did this he was inside the ethernet, and with that he possessed a ticket to any and everywhere along the intercontinental roadwork that was the virtual world.

The extended stay hotel where Elmore stayed had no way of knowing this, but hidden within remote and secret spots throughout the facility were installed several additional towers that helped to bolster the speed and power of internet access for one room housed within the hotel—the room occupied by the now former night custodian of Saint Francis Hospital. These towers, along with some other neat little toys, helped Elmore to connect to satellite signals and GPS frequencies used by high level federal agents and military personnel, and were of course off limits to average civilians. Between these and the laptop—decked to the nines with dozens of stolen top-tier custom hardware parts—and Elmore was all set for doing some major damage if he were so inclined.

But the only bit of damage Elmore had wanted to do today had to be stalled for a bit, for despite all the bravado he exhibited over the phone with Mister Christopher Elmore hadn't the first clue as to where to begin his initial search regarding his target, one Michael Liebowitz.

Even after so many years spent obsessing over his rival—the prototypical man-giant, the ever-fresh freak against God and nature—there wasn't much insofar as concrete information on an orphan-turned jarhead-turned enforcer was concerned. Mike and Elmore naturally didn't keep in touch after they both aged out of the orphanage, and there were only maybe half a dozen times over the years where a body could stomach the time and energy to actively look into the current goings-on of the man who'd done him bad as a child. Until now Elmore Johnson had been doing all he can to avoid thinking of Michael Liebowitz, but considering the near-constant nightmares and the flashbacks and the eternal hate there hasn't been much luck on suppressing the demon thoughts.

The orphanage where they both lived as kids closed down not long after they went out and did their own thing, so that avenue wouldn't be much more than a dead end at this point. Both men had served in the military, but Elmore had already looked into Mike's service record one time before and knew that there wasn't much there that could be of some use to him. His number was unlisted; Mike's calling capacity was possibly nothing more than a string of burner phones one right after another, to keep from the feds tracking his movements—this was just standard procedure for criminal enforcers and their colleagues. The house was bought and paid for, with cash, and Mike took off from there this morning after an altercation with a neighbor. The truck had also been paid for with cash, and there was no guarantee that Mike didn't ditch the vehicle or take it to a chop shop to be repainted and given some plates.

With no other recourse for gathering intel, Elmore opted for the unthinkable and decided upon accessing Mister Christopher's encrypted business files on his network. Ordinarily a man wouldn't dare to do such a thing against a boss as good as Mister Christopher had been to Elmore, but as this was now a critical situation a man had to do any last ditch effort in order to garner a shred of help in getting the job done.

It took Elmore only a few minutes to break into the network, and from there just a few minutes more to locate the files pertaining to Michael Liebowitz, also known as 'Big Mike.' The first file included a full body and face picture of the beast, and Elmore took a sudden intake of breath in shock over just how big Mike turned out to be in adulthood. The size he was when he was ten years old did nothing to hint at the size he was now—from looking at him one wouldn't be stretching the truth too far to call him an incredible hulking figure, a walking timebomb, an avatar for destruction and a volcano in human form.

A picture is worth a thousand words, and the picture on file showing Mike Liebowitz overshadowed the scant description that accompanied it. Mike would be hell to deal with, of this Elmore was certain.

Elmore did some more digging around in the files regarding his prey, and he kept reading despite the lingering urge to quench his thirst with another beer or three. The detailed reports concerning Mike and his partner Johnny Gunn were thorough, and they suggested an excellent if trigger-happy partnership. Putting the squeeze on storefront operators who didn't pay out on protection money was only the beginning of the kind of work they did—over time the two men built up a solid reputation as among Mister Christopher's top underlings. The job they did in Tokyo, managing to triple an initial investment on narcotics while only wasting two or three guys in the process, was truly remarkable.

Why they went no higher than chief enforcers at this point made no sense to Elmore. It boggled the mind why men such as these would rise through the ranks, only to stop at upper mid-management, hinted at something being amiss. The question was what.

Then after a few moments the answer appeared before him in the form of a small report detailing a problem with some illegally obtained foreign cars which were then brought into the States. From the report it seemed that the captain heading the ship holding the cars had wanted to strong-arm Mister Christopher's men into paying him a higher percentage of the profits after the individual cars were sold off (Mister Christopher wasn't present for this particular meeting). What's more, he wanted his share in advance, meaning he wanted the money before the cars could even be sold off or chopped for parts. He'd gotten a little big for his britches after a string of good luck had fattened his pockets during a stint in Egypt, and he thought he could throw his weight around and bully some stupid Americans into giving in to what he wanted.

One thing led to another, and before anyone realized what was happening Big Mike took exception to the ship captain calling him an oversized freak. Elmore could feel the blood flow from his chilled face as he read the details concerning the rampage that the big lug went on after being called such a name. He grew cold as he'd begun drawing connections between what the man-giant did to those men and what the boy-giant did to him many years ago, in the back yard of the orphanage. The destruction to life and property didn't stop until the threat of feds raining down and putting the screws to everybody involved loomed over them; the people who represented the Syndicate along with

Mike and Johnny were lucky to come out of the situation alive, and it took Mister Christopher an extra three weeks just to finalize the deal before he lost any more money on it.

Holy mother of God, Elmore thought to himself as he tried to recover from what he just read. *This man has the soul of a devil inside him. This goes far beyond being a freak—this is downright demonic!*

Elmore started to read some more of the file on Mike (who he'd started to refer to as the hellhound in his own mind), and he continued to read until he reached another entry that caught his eye, created just days prior. This one concerned a topic that Elmore hadn't even considered, and it shook him harder than the previous thing he'd read, concerning Mike's rampage. The note in question concerned the man-giant's parentage—specifically, it details Mike's father, David Liebowitz, now going by the name of Lieber, is alive and well, and currently serving as the sheriff of Chase City Virginia. He now walks around under Mister Christopher's employ, and Mike has no idea that this man even exists.

Upon reading this new information Elmore was flooded with a plethora of mixed emotions. At this point he could no longer resist the craving, and he had to run over to the fridge and grab up some beers before his insides began to claw their way out and take in some air.

Stopping at the fridge with the door half open, his hand dangling over a Tall Boy, Elmore considered the knowledge that had been dropped on him like a hurricane over some coastal town. This sheriff of Chase City was very much alive, and he is in a roundabout way working for the same man that his son worked for up until the night prior. And yet according to the report Mister Christopher had known about this for some but chose to keep it a secret, withholding it from even his top enforcer—this stood out as the most awesome and twisted fact to come up in all the history of organized crime so far as Elmore Johnson was concerned. This piece of information wasn't just important though; this fact could very well be the germ of a seed, which in turn could grow into the beginning stages of a plan for revenge. All Elmore would have to do was to drive down to Chase City and have a talk with this David Liebowitz—now named Lieber—and then from there the rest of the plan would develop into a beautiful tapestry of bloodshed and destruction.

Thus sustained by the starting sprouts of desire, Elmore laughed as he grabbed the Tall Boy from out of the fridge and pulled the tab. He toasted himself and took the can to his lips, draining the precious oat-derived liquid from out of it in the span of six seconds. After finishing this one he went ahead and grabbed another, feeling the need to continue celebrating the good fortune of finally having some of the puzzle pieces fall into place.

It would only be a matter of time until the other pieces would fall as well.

CH. 9: AND SPEAKING OF FATHERS...

Mike pulled out from the underground road and took a two hour drive into Chase City, as this was the first random spot he could think of where he and Johnny could hide out from the Richmond police for a bit. While they did this they could consider their next course of action for stealing some quick money and building up a neat little nest egg that could last them the next few days at least.

"When are we gonna get something to eat?" Johnny asked, suddenly waking up from his restless slumber inside the passenger seat. He'd been asleep from five minutes after Mike gunned out from the garage, and only just now could be bothered to join the land of wakefulness. "I haven't eaten since the Waffle House, and my gut's starting to bark at me."

"We'll eat when we eat," Mike said, eyeing the line of gas stations they were blowing past. "Right now I'm trying to figure our next move."

"Our next move should be to stop at Gino's around the corner and get some food," Johnny said. He began fiddling with the pack in his shirt pocket, making for his lighter in his pants with his free hand. "I heard from a friend who used to live around here that they make a good slice."

"We'll see about getting a slice after we do a job," Mike

stated, pulling out onto Main Street and watching for the midday traffic. He cut off the radio and rolled down the window, listening to the sounds of a quiet town that was barely breathing, being made to survive off the humming respirator of government funding and the kindness of one's Baptist neighbors.

"We do a job in a town as small as this and we won't be able to even go to Gino's," Johnny whined. He stopped fiddling with his lighter and sunk deeper into his seat. "We do a job here and we'll have to gun it out of town to keep from catching fire from the local fuzz."

"Ok then, we'll get our food down the road," Mike retorted. "Once we get a little money we'll have plenty of time to nab a quick lunch."

"This is bull," Johnny muttered, barely loud enough to be heard by a common fly.

"What was that?" Mike demanded. His attention was lightning-quick, given over completely to his partner.

Johnny cleared his throat, and spoke louder. "I said that this is bull. It is pure grade-A bill, and you know it to be true. We should be eating by now. I should be stuffing my face with slice after slice of pepperoni pizza, stuffed to the gills with layers of gooey cheese. Top it off with a few gallons of beer and I'll be set for life."

"You have a worse appetite than I do," Mike remarked. "And in any case I thought this whole stupid mess was your idea. I was the one who let you talk him into it. There's no way you're gonna turn around and act a fool just because you wanna give your bowels reason to complain."

"Can we just hurry up and figure something out before I die in this dub truck of yours? I'm about ready to pop at any moment, and I don't want my last moments to be stuck in here with you and arguing over food down the main drag of Chase City VA."

"I tell you what," Mike said. "Let's see where the police station's at."

"What? Why are we going to the police station? Don't tell me my hunger is reason enough for you to have me booked and processed." Johnny contorted his face and fell immediately into his schtick. Mike could never tell whether Johnny was for real when he fell into his schtick.

"Shut up and quit acting like an idiot. I swear, you act worse than I do when I get hungry. Seriously, I don't understand why you don't get a basic concept."

"Don't talk trash to me Mike. You need to tell me why we're going to the police station instead of hitting up a restaurant for some pizza. Sometimes you don't make any sense, and right now you're making no sense at all."

"Look you nimrod, it's real simple. We're gonna break into a couple of cop cars and swipe the radio equipment. The country cops are more laid back than the city police; they're too dumb to know what hit them, even if we do it in the broad daylight."

"What if some random townie walks by while we're raiding the cars?" Johnny asked.

Mike found the police station and turned down the alley street between the building and a line of small businesses, stacked one against the other. He parked the truck behind some dumpsters and turned to Johnny, raising his jacket to reveal his handgun stowed away in its holster.

"We find some hillbilly that wants to stir up trouble," Mike said, and we lay him to rest for his trouble." His smile had the menace of the Plague.

Johnny shook his head. "I'm starting to wish I thought this thing over a time or two before giving you the idea. I'll be the first to admit that I didn't work through any of the details when I first thought of it."

"That's right you didn't work through the details," Mike snorted. "You never work through the details, of anything. That's why I always have to pick up the slack and pull your sorry butt out of the fire."

Johnny wanted very much to bring up the times when

Mike was the one who got them into the fire to begin with, but he thought better of it. He knew that to bring up the past would only invite more trouble, and considering the by-the-pants approach they'd opted to take there wasn't any room for more trouble than had already come with the territory. Instead of touching on a sore subject Johnny sighed, opened the passenger door and got out of the truck, not saying another word.

Mike cut off the engine, pulled the key out of the ignition, opened the driver side door and struggled to climb out of the cab. Once he was out he took extra care in keeping it down as he shut the door behind him. This done, he opened the tool box up against the back window of the truck, and dug around till he found the hangers and supplies for breaking into any car a man could want to break into. Some of these things Mike has had since he and Johnny first started out—why he still carried them around was anybody's guess. Probably for sentimental reasons, as they called back to a simpler time in life, when a heart wasn't so hardened to the realities of the world.

In any case Mike was glad to still have them in his possession. Like a good Cub Scout, a man was always prepared for anything.

Johnny took the tools from Mike and they began to walk around into the back lot of the police station, where they had the pick of five squad cars that were currently stationed one after the next. Mike chose the last one toward the edge of the lot that was closest to where the truck was parked. In less than a couple minutes they'd jiffy-rigged their way into the driver side, and were halfway to pulling out the CB and stereo equipment (among other valuable things).

It was at this moment, as Mike was beginning to hand the bulk of the stuff from the first vehicle over to Johnny, that a set of boots had started to stumble down the stairs from the back door of the station. The boots belonged to a pair of long, shaking legs, which in turn belonged to a rather short torso and a pair of knotted arms. Setting on top of this cobbled-together mess of a body was a head, about the shape and texture of a ripe onion, fitted with a Stetson hat and a pair of shades.

The man's beige-colored uniform shirt had a patch stitched to the sleeve, which read CHASE CITY POLICE DEPARTMENT, SHERIFF'S OFFICE. Over the heart rests a badge, and over the badge rests the pin-on name tag which reads DAVID LIEBER, SHERIFF.

The man's given name had originally been Liebowitz, but when he came rolling into town more than twenty years ago he chose to mask his Semitic heritage. Previous experience stemming from a biker gang three towns over proved to David that to be an out and proud Jewish man among the immediate world of white "Christians" would be unwise. Why he thought that joining in with a rural county police force would be a smart decision, David hadn't a clue.

The years on the job took their toll on both the body and the mind, and the mind didn't need any help in eroding on itself after the first wife died while giving birth to a 12-pound baby. The second wife added her own brand of stress on the man, demanding he give up the child before he was a year old and talking right; from that moment on the man who would become the Sheriff of Chase City had been forced to live a life where one decision after the next had been made by someone other than him. Even the choice to take bribes from the Syndicate out in Richmond was not his to make, but had been made for him by powers grander than his own.

Was it any wonder that the abundance of beer and whiskey David drank every morning before work was beyond the grasp of his control?

David crept out the back door of the station in order to sneak a few nips of the whiskey he brought with him in one of the many flasks he hid around the place. He wanted just one nip, or maybe even five nips, to calm his nerve and stop the shaking in his hands, because the mayor was going to be coming through later on in the day and he wanted to look semi-presentable when she stopped by. Knowing that his job was on the line, David understood the gravity by which everything had to be in perfect working order, held together by a fine and delicate balance.

Which made the sight of two men stealing equipment out of cop cars all the more infuriating to the man behind the badge, with a righteous gun holstered next to where he kept his flask.

"Hold it," Sheriff Dave called out, putting up a hand as if it were the end-all, be-all weapon to put an end to all crime. "Boys, I would like to have a talk with you inside this here station if you don't mind. You mind bringing that equipment over here to me for a moment?"

Mike and Johnny stopped what they were doing and turned to face the sheriff. They stood in their original spot and held onto the equipment, looking as though they were considering whether to cut and run or to stay and work through it. Dave eyed them both and couldn't help but laugh.

Maybe it was the whiskey talking through his veins, but in that moment Sheriff Lieber had an idea pop into his head. Emboldened by the idea, the sheriff puffed out his chest and spoke up again.

"Gentlemen, I'd be happy to make a deal with you right now. I'll let you boys go, with not one lick of trouble, so long as you provide me with a little fat for my coin purse. The question I have to ask you is this: how much is your freedom worth?"

It was at that moment that David gave Mike a good and honest look, the effect of which gave his body a bit of a shake. "Now hold on a minute," he said, his bony chest deflating back to nothing as he started losing steam. You look familiar boy—who is it that you work for?"

Mike's eyes widened, as he looked from David to Johnny, and then from Johnny back to David. "What's that again?" he asked, after an extended moment of contemplation.

David shook his head. "You a little hard of hearing son? Or is ya just slow?" He turned to Johnny and pointed back to Mike. "Your friend seems a trifle dumb. Can't pick at the uptake none at all."

Johnny kept his mouth shut, and shrugged his shoulders like that was ample enough answer and the sheriff could just take it or leave it.

"Well glory be. I guess we have two slant-eyed idiots to tend to here." Sheriff Dave snorted, walking closer to the would-be thieves. "If I'd a son that I knew anything about I would've told him to stay in school so as not to turn out to be a freak much like the two's of you."

And before Sheriff Dave could complete his next step across the lot, Mike maneuvered the junk in his hands around, snatched his gun from the holster, aimed and shot the sheriff dead between the eyes.

Johnny barely had time to react as Mike tucked his gun back into its holster just as fast as he pulled it out, turning to him as he said, "Let's take what we've got and find a place to unload it somewhere in Buckingham. It's out of the way, but I know for a fact there are plenty of dopes just itching to give quick cash for goodies like this."

With the next course of action thus laid out in such minute detail, Mike ran for the truck, with Johnny tailing close behind them. They climbed into cab and shoved the stuff into the back, and then Mike started the engine, shifted gears and tore off for a side road before any one of the deputies could come out of the station and see what all the noise was about.

Sheriff David Lieber, formerly David Liebowitz, was dead before he hit the ground. The last thought that entered through his head before the bullet went through it was to ask himself why this monstrosity of a man who stood before him looked so familiar. The simple answer to that would have astounded both men, had they but taken the time to explore the mystery. As it stood now neither of them had the chance to appreciate the gravity of it, or much of anything else.

CH. 10: BOSS DROPS THE BALL

Robert had been fielding calls—many excruciating calls—for the last several hours, and he was growing more frustrated with every successive call. The Richmond police, or rather the members of the Richmond police who were regularly receiving handouts from the Syndicate, were starting to drop the ball on everything concerning this small situation he had going on with a particular ex-employee, along with his friend and running companion. It was going to take some considerable time, manpower and resources just to head up damage control and assessment...and Robert Christopher wasn't interested in spending any more of any of those things than was absolutely necessary. Less, if he was able to.

The only man who was pulling his own weight on this matter, it would seem, was Officer Grubbs...or Grabb...or whatever his name was...and Robert was going to remember him well in the near future. This kid was going to be going places, and the man who built up the Syndicate out from nothing was sure to want to turn him into something special within the organization.

Of course a man had to be careful when doing something like that. There was a time not so long ago when another kid showed promise, learning the ropes and climbing through the ranks like there was nothing to them. That kid had the talent, the flair, the muscle, and even the occasional bout of brilliance that truly shined in a company such as this. And Robert Christopher noticed well enough to shower the kid with praise, honor, and the kind of loyalty that is shown upon only the closest of relatives, like a son or a first nephew.

That kid turned out to be Michael Liebowitz, aka 'Big Mike', and he was starting to turn sour like a really bad egg. Somebody has managed to break into the hen house and corrupt the produce; a man had to get to the bottom of it before the whole farm had to be gutted, strip-searched, and left to heap mountains of ash upon itself.

So while Robert was talking on the phone with Officer Grubbs, or Grabb, or whatever his name was, He was sure to heap on the praise and accommodations. He lavished him with promises of a pay bonus, and women, and drinks imported from the far reaches of the Orient. He did with the new man the same as he did with any man who showed early promise—only he didn't offer him a seat within the inner circle. Not yet at least, not unless he could be sure of a few things first.

"Keep up the good work my man," Robert said into the phone as he was coming to the end of his final call. "I'll be sure to talk with some of your higher-ups, let them know what an honorable anchor you are to the brotherhood. Both your own brothers and mine. Thank you, thank you...thank you so much, and I will talk with you later." Then he hung up and eased back into his seat, sighing as he dropped his shoulders quicker than a child drops the cookie jar once he's been caught.

"How could I have let it come to this?" Robert asked himself, after a long and brooding silence. "How could I have allowed this kingdom I built—with no more than a few grand of my dead father's money—to run the risk of being toppled over by no-good punks? They all come in and gain my trust. They take every ounce of my respect and admiration. And then they threaten to damn me in my own house. How can I—"

Robert's self-indulgent monologue was interrupted by the roaring ring of the telephone.

"Oh, to hell with the world," Robert grumbled, picking up the phone. "Whaddaya want?" he shouted into the receiver. "I'm in no mood for any more bad news. I can't stomach it without a hot meal or a cold drink to soothe me over."

"Hello Mister Christopher," said a clear masculine voice with a rural twang into the phone. "This is Deputy Bohnefeld, with the Chase City Sheriff's Office. I found your calling cards in Sheriff Lieber's personal effects? The card said that you were to be called immediately if a problem were to arise."

Robert nearly bolted from his seat. "*Personal effects?* Is Liebowitz dead?"

"I don't know a Liebowitz sir. This is Sheriff Lieber we're talking about. Are you feeling ok sir? Is your phone connection obstructed in any way?"

Robert seethed at the casual disrespect inherent in Deputy Bohnefeld's remarks. This must have been some new kid, one with whom Robert hadn't yet had the chance of sinking his hooks into. But Robert was also instantly mad with himself, for in his exasperation he let the sheriff's true name slip with someone who clearly wasn't in the know, and he would need to recover pretty quick if he was to get out of the potential trap he'd set for himself.

"Are you there Mister Christopher? Hello?" The voice on the other end didn't even change in tone, and showed no hint of emotion beyond an hypnotic robotic hum. It barely resonated with Robert, and it took him another moment to realize he'd drifted off into his own reflective thoughts.

"Oh yes, sorry deputy," Robert said, only all too happy to recover from his slight misstep. "I must have been thinking of somebody else. Too many guys named David running through my head. Now you say that the sheriff is dead, and of course you were about to tell me whether it was of natural causes. I'd just spoken with him only recently, so this has me in for a shock as you can imagine."

"It definitely wasn't a natural death," said the deputy. "Lieber was shot in the head at point blank range. We have no idea who did it; the truck drove off before anybody had a chance to come out and see who'd done it."

"If you didn't see the vehicle, then how'd you know it was a truck?"

"We could hear the roar of a diesel engine from inside the station. It was clear as day and twice as loud as the gunshot what came before it."

"Woah woah woah woah," Robert said, getting up from his chair. "Now lemme just get something straight here. You heard the gunshot from inside the station, as well as the roar of a truck engine. Yet you couldn't get out of the building quick enough to catch sight of the man or the vehicle he was driving? I don't mean to sound any type of way son, but just what sort of cop are you?"

"I'm not your son," the deputy said. "Please don't call me that. I just thought you should know so that you could get in touch with his girlfriend and tell her the situation. I would do it myself, but I've got the investigation to conduct. And besides it would be a little complicated, seeing as he's got a wife who doesn't know he likes running around." And with that Bohnefeld hung up, leaving Robert to sit there and stew in the glory of professional incompetence on the part of county policemen.

Cradling the phone for a brief eternity, Robert began to pace the floor as he inspected every crack running the length and width of the ceiling. He ran a through figurative measures in his head to clear his mind, praying against all the odds to become calm and collected in short order. This was a new technique culled from a score of self-help books and spiritual lectures that Robert was trying, every one of them digested for the sole purpose of making him a more effective leader. Over the recent years he was beginning to feel as though there was something missing from his life as well as the command of his company, and he wanted to do everything possible to rectify that. In the present moment he wondered if any of it had been worth the time and energy.

After several minutes of rushed meditation, Robert replaced the receiver back into the dock and eased down into his chair. This new problem of the sheriff being killed had only served to wake the soul of a man up, and with eyes wide open Robert was seeing clearly just how screwed he was by not paying careful attention to the people he employed.

Of course it had to have been Mike and Johnny involved in this killing. The mention of a diesel engine brought to mind Mike's stupid truck, the massive tank of metal that Mike just had to have once he had gotten tired of feeling cramped in the classic Chrysler sedan he was driving around in. It couldn't have been anybody else, and if Mike was involved then surely his old pal Johnny Gunn was close by. And if Johnny Gunn was close by then there was sure to be more in the works which could serve to further complicate matters. Which if all of this true then these men were due for more punishment than they were already bringing on themselves over several recent miscarriage of duties, not the least of which was the way that Mike had done in the who brought in the cars and Johnny stood back and basically watched it happen. That the sheriff was actually Mike's father was only more fuel for the fire, and now that the sheriff was dead Robert couldn't even use this knowledge as leverage against his former employee.

Unless.

Yes, that was it. All Robert had to do was get a hold of

Mike, along with his buddy Johnny, and let him know a couple of things he may not have known about himself. A couple of things which may bring a mountain of a man to his knees. If the Boss-Man could do that to the Big Guns; then a man can begin to pick up the slack that had been developing for so long. It was a simple enough plan, and for a second Robert had considered getting back in touch with the loser Elmore and coordinate with his efforts to locate the man he had every reason to hate as well.

But just as quickly as he'd thought that particular thought, Robert just as quickly cast it aside. Better let the loser do his own work, and not give him any more help than he was already getting (which was as good as none). There was too great a risk in allowing an underling to get so close to him; Mike was evidence enough that the risk of going south would drop on your head in the space of a breath. It was best to keep Elmore at a distance for now, and therefore be free enough to sick the dogs on him at the first glimpse of a problem.

Robert Christopher had made one too many mistakes with the men who'd worked under him. He realized this now. But with a little work and some good planning, maybe it wasn't too late to fix the cracks before the walls come crumbling to his feet. And with this burst of encouragement Robert reached for the top drawer of his desk, pulled it open, reached in and grabbed the keys to his Dodge Charger. He was going to drive himself for this next stage in the plan that was forming in his mind as he went along, and he wasn't going to let anyone know what he was doing.

It was best for a man to start doing everything himself, and not tell anyone what was happening till it was all was said and done. That way the taste of victory could be savored, and the bragging would be so much better.

And besides, even if it were all to fail anyway Robert still had one unspoken failsafe. The one thing, his ace in the hole, was his ticket—just in case he needed it. Should he need to cash it in, Mike would then feel the pain of betrayal. Then Robert can sweep in and make his move.

CH. 11: WHAT ARE WE GONNA DO NOW?

"I need to go ahead and eat something before I pass on for the grave," Johnny shouted from over the blaring sounds of country that was coming out of the speakers. "We left that sheriff dead on the ground back there, and now we're going out of our way into Buckingham without even bothering to check whether somebody saw us."

"Nobody saw us," Mike said, interrupting Johnny. He was driving down yet another po-dunk dirt road, his hands tense on the wheel as he did everything he could to keep the tires from running off into the ditch at either side. "I did a quick once-over before we left. There wasn't a soul in sight. We got out of that one-horse town with the speed that many hundreds of horsepower can provide to us. Those hick cops won't even know what hit em come morning."

"Yeah, I'm sure they won't. I am certain that Mister Christopher never once bothered with having a man or two working on the Chase City force. And I am glad to find comfort in the knowledge that not one of those men will be calling him up to give the news regarding a fellow man in uniform—a *paid* man in uniform mind you, one who's been bought out by dirty money—being gunned down by a walking time bomb. I swear Mike, I should have just said my goodbyes and let you drive off into the sunset this morning. It's getting later and later in the day as it is, and all we've done was to ensure our tickets to the grave show, with our corpses being the main attraction."

"You need to learn to shut up," Mike said, with the emotional range of a bot.

"You need to learn not to lay into every man that calls you a freak," Johnny snorted back.

"Piss off with that one my brother. You've known that was my trigger from the first week we worked together. Don't start holding that against me now that we're caught in a small bind."

"I'll hold it against you if I want to Mike. This is getting ridiculous. I just wanted to grab up some quick cash to hold me over till I come back from off my vacation, and I wanted to have you work it with me for the sake of being friends. But from the moment we broke off this morning you've been going with a wild hair stuck up somewhere, and now that we're on the job it's been nothing but a series of asking for inches and taking miles."

Mike shook his head. "You don't make no sense talking about inches and miles. And in any case it's not a vacation if you're gonna be working a bunch of small jobs while you're on it." He then flashed his turn signal and began pulling into a small truck stop and diner just up ahead. "I'm gonna go ahead and stop in here. We can get something to eat, and you can quit your complaining for an hour—if you can manage it."

"Oh, so now we're going to eat? Because you say so? Well, isn't that just great!" Johnny double-pounded the dash board, both hands opened to the palm. "I'm so sick of having you call all the shots, just because you're the biggest bully in town!"

"I'm not the biggest bully in town," Mike said. Again, no emotion.

"Yes Mike. Yes you are the biggest bully in town. Maybe along the whole coast even. I bet you can't name one person, not one that stands throughout all of human history, who can outclass you in the bullying department."

Mike pulled into a parking spot, shifted into park, cut off the engine, and then looked at Johnny dead in the eye, and said, "I can think of at least one. Anybody can think of at least one guy who's a bigger pain than I am."

He and Johnny sat in the truck for the next several moments, staring at each other in silence. The issue of bullying had come up only once before during the course of their friendship, and it was just as awkward the first time as well. This second time they had the added frustration of both a car job gone awry and a dead sheriff weighing down the air with the stench of a moral dilemma. These were not the sorts of things that men of the criminal fraternity needed on their souls, no matter how far up the ladder of said fraternity.

Finally, after the air inside the cab had gotten too thick with stifled masculine rage, Johnny decided to speak first. Clearing his throat, he said, "Well if we're going to eat we might as well make it quick. Got enough stolen police equipment in here to cause us trouble should someone try and snoop around on us."

"I was gonna try and unload the stuff before we did anything else," Mike said. "But you wouldn't stop with your nagging lips and the tapeworm that's stuck to your gut."

"A man who eats five burgers in a single sitting wants to accuse me of having a tapeworm is rich. He's millionaire-level rich I tell you."

"Let's just get inside and grab a quick meal. I'll settle up the tab for ya."

"Oh, I was expecting for you to settle up the tab anyways."

"And that, my friend, is what I'd like to call millionaire-level rich. Wanna go for a couple of specials in here?"

"Sure. Would be too good a deal not to go for the special. I feel bad for the restaurant though. They're gonna lose out on the deal."

"I don't feel bad at all. Makes me sick to try to feel bad."

They got out of the truck together, ready to dig in on truck-stop quality cuisine.

>>>

"We got a steak, medium rare, with green beans and fries for the guy at table seven!" shouted Monica through the window. "And if I can get that order of pancakes out to table nine before next year that'll be great!"

"Calm your voice when you talk to me girl," Charlie called back, smirking at Monica through the window from his spot at the grill. "It wouldn't sound good for you to be talking to me that way before we get the chance to roll out on our date tonight. Think I'd wanna bring you home to momma when you're acting that way to me beforehand?"

"I'm taking you home from work because your car dropped its transmission," Monica said. "We are not going on a date, and you are certainly not taking me home to momma." Even as she said the words she couldn't help but laugh. "Hand me the food when you're done with it hon. Ok thanks, I love you so much!" And with that she turned and walked off to serve her other tables, leaving Charlie to stare at her through the frame of the call-through window.

Dang those Hebrew girls are fine, Charlie thought to himself, as he went back to placing the butter on top of the pancakes before sending them off into the world.

And the truth was that Monica Sedaris knew very well just how fine she was. It was only that she didn't care, and she would have preferred if Charlie and every other man who came into her path didn't care either. Her shoulder-length brown hair, curled so perfectly that she daren't straighten it, served to surround her angular face like a halo. Her skin was tanned to a smooth olive finish, and her nose pointed in such a fashion that it seemed to point to her pouting lips as well as her eyes, which were a shade of brown not unlike the shifting autumn leaves. Of course men like Charlie were quick to notice her figure, thin but with the added bonus of sleek curves that were not well hidden underneath her khaki pants and work shirt. Her wiry, 5' 5" frame seemed a touch short to some people, but for most it seemed a perfect frame to house a perfect angel, cast unto the earth from heaven for some unknown purpose by God Himself.

Monica realized all of this, and found that she'd wanted none of it. She was in her mid-twenties and was set to finish her degree from Union Seminary (the one in Richmond, not in New York). A Messianic Jew, she converted from her Orthodox faith with her mother after her father died. From the moment she first entered the sanctuary of the Presbyterian church down the road from her house, she felt this odd calling tugging at her heartstrings that told her of some other profession than the nothingness which she had been forced to hold ever since she could remember. This calling manifested itself when she first set foot on campus of community college, where she took an introductory class on religion to fulfill a gen-ed requirement.

That first class, taught by a recent doctoral graduate in comparative religions, had led Monica to take every class the school offered on religion, including the admittedly shallow courses on both the Old and the New Testaments. She graduated from John Tyler Community College with an associate's degree (plus a few extra credits on her new pet subject), and when she went on to study at William & Mary she double-majored in both English and Religious Studies. Thus equipped with such a rich and multi-layered background, Monica still felt a lingering hunger, an appetite for something that she could not quite name but for which she had yet to find the stuff adequate to feed it.

Then the associate pastor at the Presbyterian church had recommended that she consider attending Union Seminary, where he'd just finished his Master's in Theology with a concentration in church history. The young man, full of scripture and exegetical passion, was quick to offer his guidance and support to the academically gifted Monica, until the time came when he could no longer hide his own longing for a woman whose physical beauty appeared to him as an act of miraculous affection. He made his affections known, and the fallout between man and woman was soon to follow.

But though Monica Sedaris no longer spoke to the young minister, still she continued with her studies at the seminary. The classes on liturgy and doctrine were of particular interest to her, and she whipped through every course with a frenzy unequalled by any of her fellow classmates. She was nearing the end of her studies now, only a semester away from completing her Masters and considering a Doctorate in Church History. Several of her professors were only all too willing to provide letters of recommendation and any other help that they could provide. Monica was grateful to them all, but the young seminarian was experience enough to caution her not to so readily accept assistance from any man.

She even was willing to help a man if she could, as evidenced by her offering to Charlie home after work. But with this she still managed to keep a cool distance, for she had not yet found a man who could ignite within her the fires of love equal to that which she possessed for the reaches of higher learning. Until a man can do that, he can just keep away for the time being.

Monica had just taken the plate of pancakes from the window (put up a few seconds before by Charlie) and brought it to her customer. She was just about to grab the pot of coffee and refill some mugs when Mike and Johnny walked in. She caught sight of Mike first as they were making their way to a table—how could she not, as big as he was—and she stopped out in the middle of the restaurant floor. When Mike turned halfway to face her and sat in the booth, Monica lost her breath for a few moments, as well as nearly lose her grip on the pot she was holding. She managed to catch herself in time to keep from dropping it, but the effect of it still lingered in front of her.

The man was impossibly big; that much was obvious. He had to have been seven feet tall, and with shoulders that reached halfway across the length of the booth as he sat down. How someone had managed to find the fabric to construct a suit to cover a body like that, Monica hadn't a clue. But he was sitting there, clear as day, and all Monica would have to do was trust her eyes and know that this impossibility of a man did in fact exist.

The man had skin that was dark like hers, and hair that was coarse like sand. Monica couldn't tell with 100 percent certitude, but from where she stood looking at him it would appear that he was of a Jewish background, just like her. One thing was certain: his face held the rugged good looks of a man who held the weight of all the world's tragedy behind his eyes.

If a soul could fall instantly in love with another, Monica was in that moment feeling the pains of such a phenomenon. She could not articulate what was suddenly filling her with euphoria, but she was secretly praying to God that she could hold it together for long enough to get through the next hour or two that this passerby and his friend would be in this building with her.

Monica quickly went around to fill all the empty coffee cups she could find and walked over to where Mike and Johnny were sitting. Setting the pot down at a nearby table, she brought out her notepad and pen, opened to a new page and asked the men, "What can I get for you gentlemen? I'm Monica, and I'll be serving you today."

"Nice to meet you Monica. The name's Mike." Mike, with the tragic eyes and coarse hair, looked up at Monica, and gave her a wry little smile that nearly broke her in two.

"Nice to meet you Mike," Monica said. She matched his

smirk with a smile of her own, and she let her eyes hang onto his for dear life.

"My name's Johnny," muttered the shorter man sitting across from the handsome giant. "I'm sitting here hungry, if anybody's interested..."

"Oh yes, I'm sorry," Monica stammered, snapping back to reality. She looked over to Johnny and smiled, though not as wide or warm as she'd smiled for Mike. "Do you know what you'd like to eat?"

"I don't know. What do you have in the burger department that's good?"

"Our bacon burger is pretty popular sir."

"The name is Johnny Gunn, not 'sir'. I know we're in Virginia, and Virginia is technically part of the south. But I won't stand for anybody to call me 'sir'. None of that bull-spit southern manners crap, you got that?"

"Yes sir—I mean, yes. Yes, I got that." Monica's face flushed as she made little glances over to Mike. "So how about it sir—I mean Johnny. Would you like one of our bacon burgers?"

"Sure thing ma'am," Johnny said, without a hint of irony. "Gimme a bacon burger, double patty, with cheddar, and cover it with everything you got. I want fries, and a Coke to drink for now. Thanks."

Monica wrote this all down as fast as she could, casting a few more glances over to Mike as she did. Once she was done she nodded to Johnny and then turned back to Mike, who only smiled to her again. "And what can I get for you sir—I mean Mike."

"I'll take the same thing he's having. And you can call me sir or whatever it is you want."

Monica blushed again as she wrote down "X2" next to Johnny's order. She looked up and matched Mike's smile. "Anything else I can get for you guys?"

"Yeah," Johnny chimed in, pulling a gun out from under the table. "Box everything up and bring us all the money you have in the register."

Monica could feel a bodily reaction hit her again as she looked up to see the gun in her face, though for different reasons than just minutes before.

>>>

"That was a good special," Johnny said in between bites of his food. He watched as Mike drove down the road with one hand on the wheel and the other hand gripping his burger. In the back along with the stolen equipment was a large paper to-go bag, stuffed to the point of overflowing with all the cash from the register.

"I cannot believe that woman back there," he continued, stopping a moment to wash his food down with a sip of his soda. Swallowing, he added, "The way she was looking at you, I would've thought she'd wanna run away and marry you."

Mike burped, collected himself and said solemnly, "Maybe in another life I would've agreed to marry a woman like her. She looked good enough to marry anyway. I don't like that we had to do what we did, but it comes with the territory."

"You said it. Now let's go and unload this equipment for some more cash. Oh, and Mike? Thanks for stopping for the food. It really means a lot."

"Sure man. No problem."

The next several miles were ridden in relative silence, save for the casual munching on food, and the sounds of Merle Haggard playing in the background. Now that he had his food Johnny didn't care what Mike played on the radio.

CH. 12: ELMORE LOSES IT

Elmore could have gotten himself going far earlier than he did, but he was so busy preemptively celebrating that he was blotted off his rocker by the time he finally decided to leave the room at the hotel. A body shouldn't be able to handle that much beer at one time, but this body in particular had somehow managed to build up a tolerance that bordered on superhuman. Which of course was precisely the problem—because the more that Elmore drank the more the drink was failing to live up to expectation. A man needed to drink in order to get over, but with so much in his system Elmore stood in constant fear of going over the edge at any moment.

These sorts of problems didn't bother Elmore all that much, however, for while he'd taken a couple of drunken detours along the way he still kept mainly on the road to seeking his grand revenge. With a gun he 'borrowed' from a neighbor at the extended stay, and the address for the Chase City police station plugged into the GPS unit in the beat-up excuse for a car, Elmore made the trek for Chase City VA, a place he'd never even thought of entering before.

Once he got into the town he was going to have to separate the sheriff from the station and from the station's nest of hillbilly cops; when he'd secured the man he was going to search out Michael Liebowitz—the long lost son—in the hopes of putting together a crooked sort of family reunion, washed in the blood and baptized in a deluge of bullets.

Being late for enacting his own plans and still so drunk that it was a wonder he could drive at all, Elmore couldn't have known that Sheriff David Lieber, formerly Liebowitz, had been shot through the head earlier in the day. He couldn't have known that the one who shot him was the same man that he so desperately wanted to get his hands on in the first place. He had no conceivable way of preparing for any of this, but he was on his way to Chase City now, oblivious to the doom and casual frustration that was awaiting him.

The ride from Jefferson Davis over into Chesterfield was a doozy, but that was the route for which Elmore felt most comfortable for making it through to Amelia and 460. By the time he got to the first sign of rural country the traffic became almost nonexistent; it was getting on later in the evening, and nearly everybody was just wanting to get home to spend time with their families. Elmore couldn't relate to that, having been alone for all his life—this marked difference between himself and the other people in his little corner of the state only filled his mind with thoughts of murderous rage as he drove out of Amelia and on into Crewe.

On a whim Elmore pulled into the Tastee Freeze in Crewe and shut off the engine. The beer was still sloshing around in his stomach, and he figured some food would settle him down a bit. He went to open the door but was having trouble with the handle sticking; after a few failed attempts he put his shoulder into it and knocked the door open with a hard drop and a push. Pain shot through his arm and neck at the point of impact, drawing a sharp cry to escape from Elmore's chapped lips.

"Oh for the love of God!" Elmore screamed, wincing as

he climbed out of the car. "Why must you be such a *bastard?*" He then stood around in the space of pavement next to his car, favoring his shoulder and muttering several harsh blasphemies under his breath.

"I swear," he said, looking up at the sky, "I ought to take my foot and shove it—"

"What're you looking to shove?" a gruff voice demanded. Elmore looked over to see a man in a torn flannel shirt and grease-covered trucker cap coming out from the entrance door to the restaurant. The man had a large to-go cup in his hand, and he was shaking it back and forth in a slow methodical fashion. His face was flush with absurd anger.

"I asked you what you were looking to shove," the man repeated, stepping out onto the sidewalk and letting go of the door. He cut an imposing figure as a monstrosity of a man, looking as though he'd be ready to tear Elmore's limbs from out of their sockets and use them as clubs to beat his face and torso to a pulpy mess. When Elmore didn't immediately answer him, he stepped off of the sidewalk and inched toward the significantly smaller man.

"You need to answer me when I'm talking to you," the man said as he got in Elmore's face. When Elmore still didn't respond the man's own face turned a deeper shade of red, and a vein bulged over his brow. "Gonna go dumb and mute on me are ya? Well ain't that cute. Guess I'd just have to give your shoulder more of a reason to hurt. What do you have to say about that? Or are you gonna keep quiet as I lay a hurting on you?"

Elmore didn't have a chance to think—he just reacted with a deep and primal instinct as he shot out his leg and kicked the man in the groin with his steel toe work shoe. The man went down hard, screaming like a madman as he grabbed painfully between his legs. He began looking blindly up at the sky, ignoring everything around him other than what was going on between his own two legs.

"What was that you said?" Elmore asked him, starting

to marvel at the crude precision of his own handiwork. "You were shouting so loud I couldn't hear nor understand you. Here, maybe this will help you..."

And with that Elmore withdrew the 'borrowed' handgun from hidden spot behind his shirt in the back of his belt. He pointed the barrel at the man's head, and then coaxed him into looking at it. "Do you see this? This is the last thing seen by any man who dares to cross me. It'll be the last thing you see before you die."

Then Elmore shot him between the eyes, jerking his hand back as fresh blood splattered onto the barrel as well as the edges of his sleeve. A shot of adrenaline shot like a dart through the body, and it took Elmore a few moments before he realized that the pain had left his shoulder completely.

Elmore wiped the blood from off the barrel with the tail of his shirt before holstering the gun back into his belt. This done, he straightened his back and walked into the Tastee Freeze. He came up to the counter and said to the cashier, "I'd like the hotdog combo, if you please. Better make it a large, because I'm starving."

It took another twenty minutes for the police to pull into the parking lot and walk in to arrest Elmore for the crime of murder. He was dipping a couple of his fries into some ketchup when they came up behind him, and he was shocked that somebody would call and snitch on him when he'd only defended himself against a man who dared to get in his face this time of day.

"You can't blame me for defending my honor can you?" he asked as they cuffed him and began reading him his rights. "You can't very well blame me. And besides, I got things to do—you can't book me until I do what has to be done."

CH. 13: A GOOD NIGHT'S SLEEP

"How much money did we make off of the stuff?" Johnny asked Mike as they entered into their room for the night. They had opted for checking into a fly-by-night motel off of the main road, not far from the store where they unloaded the stolen CB and stereo. Mike was the one who handled the negotiating and money handling; Johnny Gunn had been left out of the deal completely. He wasn't even allowed to come in—Mike had made him wait in the truck during the whole thing.

"We made enough for you not to keep asking me questions all night," Mike said. He sat on the first of the two beds in their room and started pulling off his shoes. He groaned heavily as he first removed the right shoe, and then he groaned again as he removed the left one. Then he started to wiggle his toes around to free them from getting caught inside his socks and stretch the fabric; he did this for a couple of minutes, all the while staring at the ground and smiling like a school kid.

Johnny only grew more agitated as he watched his partner amuse himself.

"You ought to know something," Johnny said, walking over to the bed on the far side of the room. "And it is this: I really don't like it when you brush me off like I'm some kind of fool. Like I keep trying to hammer into your head this whole time, the job was my idea to begin with."

"It might have been your idea," Mike said, looking up from the ground. "But I've listened to enough of your mouth today to piss me off beyond good reason. Can't you learn to shut up and trust in my instincts?"

"Maybe I can, and then again maybe I can't. That ain't the point."

"It is to me," Mike said, rising from the bed. He paced the floor for a bit, and then started squatting and stretching out his legs. He kept groaning as he did this, letting off a regular series of purring sounds. Anyone who'd listen in would think that there was a full-grown Bengal tiger in the room with them.

"You look ridiculous doing that," Johnny snorted. "You sound ridiculous too. I don't care to sit here watching and listening to you all night, so if you would can it for a while I'd appreciate it."

"Maybe I would appreciate you letting me be," Mike said. But he very quickly did stop, and in turn began to undo his clothes. He stripped down to his undershirt and britches, folding his outer clothes and placing them neatly on the dresser. With this done Mike walked over and climbed into bed, turning out the lamp setting on the night stand.

"Goodnight Johnny," Mike said after turning off the light, leaving the room in utter darkness. After a few moments Mike was snoring like a buzz saw.

Johnny got up from his bed and walked out of the room, opening the door quietly and shutting it behind him as he stepped out into the outer world. He made his way down the corridor, stopping in front of some vending machines—one filled with various assorted candy bars and the other with canned soda (all of them Coke products of a kind). Johnny dug a handful of quarters out of his pocket and plunked them into the soda machine. He then pressed the button for a root beer. The can dispensed and he grabbed it up and pulled the tab, taking the can to his lips and drinking long and hard.

Quenching his thirst, Johnny took the can with less than a quarter of the drink left and tossed it in a nearby trashcan. Then he did a quick look around to see that nobody was creeping about in the parking lot watching him. Satisfied with the knowledge that he was alone, Johnny pulled out his cell phone and dialed some numbers. He put the phone to his ear and listened to it ring until the person on the other end picked up.

"Hello boss," he said. "I know that you probably been hearing about us through the grapevine today, and I am sorry for not keeping you informed myself. I was caught under Mike this whole time, and I haven't really had a long enough moment to myself until now."

He stopped talking and listened to the voice on the other end for a little bit, grunting affirmatively with every other thing that was said to him. "I'll be hightailing it out of here in a little bit," Johnny said finally. "I gotta grab my share of the money we got from a couple of jobs and hot-wire a car so that I can leave this stink hole. By tomorrow morning Mike will be humbled and ready to come back to you, just as meek as a precious lamb. Yes sir, it'll all go down perfectly I reckon. In any case, I'll be seeing you soon. Ok then, bye boss."

Johnny hung up and put his phone back in his pocket. He figured he'd better grab his share of the money and drive off in the first available 4-door sedan in the lot. Mike won't be awake till un-up, and besides he was getting too comfortable with lashing out at the first sign of trouble while they were out working today. They'd spent countless hours running this way and that—Johnny could sense that Mike was set off to have a meltdown at any second.

Johnny really did care for his partner, but he couldn't stick his neck out for him any longer.

It was a cinch to jiffy-rig the locks on the truck, and it took no time for Johnny to grab up a spare bag and divide the money down the middle. Then Johnny thought it over for a second and decided to take all the money with him. He left just enough to keep Mike going for a little while, feeling that it was only right.

With the loot in his possession Johnny closed the door and began looking around the lot till his eyes landed on a nondescript Ford car that suited his needs just fine. It took only a few minutes for him to work his way inside the car, then to stow away the money and hot-wire it and get the engine running. In another minute Johnny was driving out of the parking lot, going at it smoothly till he was far enough away from everything to feel comfortable with sounding off at a higher speed.

As he drove he began having thoughts, chief among them being a hope that at the end of this the boss will take it easy on Mike. Going overboard with the revenge wouldn't be good for anyone—a man can only take so much on his conscience before his own betrayal against a friend will beat on him too savagely. Johnny understood just how wrong he was for what he was now doing, and he didn't want the boss to do something that could add to the wrongness of it.

Just to live with the first sin would be bad enough, without all the rest of them to drag him deeper into the lake of fire.

CH. 14: ROBERT DROPS THE AX

Robert had just gotten off the phone with Johnny when he began receiving another call. He answered it, saying, "This is Robert. I'm really busy now—is this something that can wait?"

"Hey Mister Christopher! It's Elmore! I got caught up in some foolishness, and now I'm in custody. Do you think you might could maybe bail me out, or something? I'm in a bind and I still want to finish the job you tasked me with."

"Woah there kid," said Robert, "now just slow down for a minute. Why are you in custody? This isn't another harassment charge is it? It better not be any kind of problem with illegal porn. Because I had a guy who worked for me before you doing computer work who's now serving 6 years for soliciting the kind of child stuff that could get you buried in some parts."

"Oh no Mister Christopher," Elmore said, and then he chuckled. "This is nothing like any of that stuff. No, I just shot a man who wanted to give me trouble at the Tastee Freeze out in Crewe. Pretty ordinary stuff if you ask me, and I knew you were wanting to ask anyways because you wanted to have all the information."

"What were you doing out in Crewe?" asked Robert, agitated and perplexed. "You live in Chester. Your whole base of operations is in a dump of a hotel that charges both by the week and the hour. There's no reason for you to be out in Crewe shooting people and getting arrested."

"I was on my way to Chase City, Mister Christopher. I had worked up this new angle for dealing with your Mike Liebowitz problem. Was only trying to go above and beyond what you wanted for me to do, and I guess I got sidetracked with this idiot who stepped to me as I stopped to get something to eat."

Robert rolled his eyes but maintained a cheerful demeanor as he talked into the phone. "All right, so here's what I'm going to do. I will have one of my lawyers come down there in a little while and bail you out. Then he will take you back to my offices, where you can go about finishing up any loose ends on the job I assigned you. It's really no problem—I've had to do this sort of thing for previous employees. It comes with the territory, so it really should've been a matter of me going over some of the risks before I had you work for me."

"Oh, actually, is there any way I can go ahead and drive the rest of the way into Chase City? I really have to make it there and handle this angle I had figured out for you."

"What's in Chase City that you'd have to handle? I've no pressing there, and frankly I don't see what that town has to do with the job that I gave you to do."

"It's Mike Liebowitz' father!" Elmore shouted into the phone. "His father is the sheriff in Chase City! Apparently he must've given him up after he was born, and in giving him up he led Mike into the same orphanage as me. This isn't just coincidence Mister Christopher—it was like fate brought you to me so that I can put an end to Mike and his long-lost kin for what he did to me.

"I have to be avenged Mister Christopher," Elmore continued. "A man cannot live unless he can be avenged!"

Robert let the man say his whole piece, making no noise or complaint as Elmore rattled on and on about some nonsense that would amount to nothing for anyone with a sound mind. When he finished Robert cleared his throat, and said, "Look, I understand your frustration. I will get one of my guys to come to you and take care of this. You will be handled swift and fair, you mark my words. Swift and fair, that's the bottom line."

Elmore was only all too happy with gratitude, yammering to the point of delirium as he laid on the praise. "Oh, thank you Mister Christopher! Thank you so much for all that you are and all that you do!"

"It's really no problem Elmore. Listen, I have to run now, but I'll be sure to send my best man along to handle your situation. You just hang tight and I'll take care of everything. And remember kid—guard your backside like it's the Holy Grail. Some of those creeps in that jail with you are wild degenerate monsters!"

With that Robert hung up and immediately started punching numbers into his phone. He brought the phone to his ear and listened to it ring until Johnny picked up. "Hey Johnny, I know I just spoke to you. Do you think maybe you could make the trek out to the Crewe police station? I know it's getting late, but we have a situation with one of my other guys landing himself in jail. I guess you will have to go ahead and kill him. And before you do that just let him know that the sheriff in Chase City is already dead. Let him know that Mike did it for good measure. Thanks Johnny."

Robert hung up and slid his phone back into his pocket, turning to Monica and Charlie standing together at the counter of the diner, freshly cleaned out of customers after being robbed. The cops had already come and gone by the time that Robert entered the scene—the members of the local police who weren't yet bought out were still notoriously lazy at conducting investigations. Robert figured he could get by with doing a little investigating of his own.

"I am sorry for having to interrupt our conversation

with so many phone calls. As you can see I am a busy man. What's say we get to the meat of the issue here, and I'll let you get back to your business."

Monica gave Charlie an uneasy look before turning her attention to Robert. "I don't know if I feel like talking about this anymore," she said, holding her stomach with both hands like she was undergoing gas-cramps from a bad lunch.

For a brief moment—and Robert relished the sight of this—it looked like Monica was about to tear up and cry right then and there.

"I know it must be tough," Robert said, smiling. "I don't mean to keep you spinning in circles. You and your cook here have more than plenty on your plate as it is, pardon the pun. It's just that this is an issue I would like to help you resolve, and in order to do what I can I will have to get a little information from you both. Do you think that you can help me, that I may help you in return?"

He began to leer at Monica as Charlie stepped in between Robert and her. "I am afraid we've no other information to give you right now man. We might remember something later though. There any chance we can call you sometime tomorrow? Me and Monica really have to get to our homes and recover from the day."

Robert just gave him a smile as he reached out his hand for Charlie to shake. "That is perfectly fine my man. Sorry to keep you both. I left my card on the counter there—be sure to call me tomorrow. You guys take care now, and good night."

Robert walked out of the place and towards the car, but instead of going for the driver side door her instead went to the trunk and opened it up, pulling out a 2-gallon container of gas and a packet of matches. He walked back to the restaurant and began dousing the front with gas, looking through the window at the fearful occupants still hanging about inside. He then tossed the empty container to the ground, pulled a match from the pack and struck it against the heel of his shoe. He gave the waitress and cook a brief smile through the window, offered them a little wave, and threw the match against the gas-stained door.

"May you learn to sing hymns with the angels in heaven," Robert said, grabbing up the gas container and walking away. The restaurant was soon engulfed in flames. From behind him Robert could just barely make out the bloodcurdling sounds of screams emitting from the man and woman who had been left to suffer alone, save for the shared company of each other. Robert just figured they'd have a back exit in the building and therefore could make it out of there if they really wanted to.

"Now I must kill a little time before I dare to wake the sleeping giant and threaten to make his life a walking, talking hell on earth," Robert said to the skies above, which were stained with shades of light against the dark ceiling from a combination of night and the flickering of flames.

"I let him burn me one too many times, and now it is time for me to leave his scorched body to rot into his grave," Robert continued. He couldn't help but to laugh at his own twisted thoughts as he tossed the fuel container into the trunk and closed the lid, climbing into the driver side of the car. He started the engine, put her in drive and pulled off, leaving behind one nasty mark of a crime scene and knowing full well that no one in the state would want to take him to task for what he'd done here tonight, or for what he was going to do in the morning. Such was the power of a corrupt local government and police system, with Robert at the center of the corruption.

It was funny how things work out like that.

CH. 15: IT'S GONNA BE A ROUGH MORNING

The Good Reverend Nathanial Bragg left from his hotel room just as the first flecks of sun stretched across the sky, and the first thing he did was to make for the vending machines down the way from his room. He made it to the machines and immediately began stretching his legs against the wall off to the side. He'd gotten little sleep the night before, his spine having caused him trouble off and on through the darkened hours, and he was looking forward to getting back home to his church in Tennessee as soon as possible.

Reverend Bragg had had a tough enough time getting by at the Southern Baptist Leadership conference. Four straight days of other ministers coming up to ask him how he was holding up, offering their condolences for the recent loss of his son. Bragg's wife had succumbed to cancer five years before, and so he'd already been made to know despair as he suffered this new loss alone—but now he had to receive the gentle prodding of members of the ministerial fraternity over the course of the entire conference. The scars were too fresh as it was, but these men were simply adding salt to the wounds without giving a thought to what they were doing.

God looked down with a face of sadness. Somewhere

Jesus wept.

The fact was that Reverend Bragg had lost his faith. There was just no other way to state it, for a man can no longer maintain his faith in God under the weight of so much misery. Job might still have been able to soldier on considering the circumstances, but Bragg knew in his heart that he was no Job. He was barely able to scrape by in seminary, where he did only average in his studies and even worse with human interaction. A country boy who will always be the son of a tobacco farmer no matter what he did, he could still feel the pings of inadequacy festering inside him. These of course were seeds planted by the parents of his late wife Susan; she was a honey-haired saint but Bragg could've sworn at times that her mother was a demon. With Susan's death the mother-in-law had only gotten worse, and now with her grandson gone Marion Zimmerman was on the warpath after the man she viewed as the originator of the tears and gnashing of teeth. This only exasperated the Reverend Bragg's already dwindling reserve of faith in humanity, and his faith in the Almighty was pretty well near obliterated anyway.

Why a man would still persist at ministry, when he no longer believed in the core tenants of the church, was a wonder. But Nathanial Bragg just didn't have it in him to quit. Not yet anyway. He would figure it out eventually, even if it killed him.

Bragg cast aside his dark thoughts for a moment as he put some change into the soda machine and selected an orange-flavored Fanta. He got his drink from the dispenser and pulled the tab; taking the can to his lips, he drank heavily the sweet nectar of carbonated processed sugar. Bragg knew better than to overdo it with the sweet stuff—he was borderline diabetic as it was, and could stand to shed a few dozen pounds to boot—but on a morning like this he simply couldn't resist the temptation. Having never been the one for regularly eating breakfast, Nathanial Bragg knew that this one 12-ounce can was going to last him until noon at the earliest. So the Good Reverend was going to enjoy his soda, and a mountain of rebukes be heaped upon the head of anyone who would dare criticize his choice.

As he drained his soda (and considered buying another) Bragg turned to face the parking lot. It was at that moment he noticed one thing that seemed immediately off—being that his Ford sedan wasn't where he'd parked it the evening before, next to a large diesel 4x4 with and off-kilter paint job and some "Don't Tread On Me" license plates. As odd as the paint job looked to the eye Bragg didn't much care; his thoughts were elsewhere, and quickly turning from simply depressed to slightly murderous.

I'll be sure to add this on my list of reasons to harm you God, the Reverend Bragg prayed thoughtfully. *I'll be sure to magnify my actions a thousand fold, and level mountains with my rage. You won't be able to handle me when I'm done, and by then I'll be coming after your flock.*

And with that Bragg walked down to the front office, hoping to see if anyone on staff would have something to drink that was stronger than soda from out of the vending machine. If Jesus could turn water into wine, then the Good Reverend felt justified in having some Jack Daniels, or even a few bottles of Budweiser if they were available.

>>>

Mike woke from a restful sleep to find that Johnny wasn't in the other bed. The other bed didn't even look like it had been slept in, and that raised Mike's suspicions. He raised himself out of bed and went to the dresser, pulling on his clothes without a single thought given to whether he was wrinkling them by being a little rough in tugging at them. The mere fact that Johnny wasn't in bed, sleeping like a baby as per usual, was enough to rattle the cages.

"You in the bathroom Johnny?" Mike called out as he zipped his pants and slid his feet into his shoes. "I don't hear you in there, so I'm gonna assume you're not trying to make." When he didn't hear anything from out of the bathroom he rolled his eyes. "Stupid jerk," he muttered. "Not like we're in the middle of a string of jobs and the clock's ticking with the boss possibly breathing down our necks. What a mess I'm in all right."

I'm in a mess that you put me in, Mike thought to himself, *and you ain't even here this morning. Figures.*

Mike walked out of the room, with his shirt still unbuttoned, and stepped out into the sidewalk. He eyed the truck from the passenger side, noticing the door left slightly open. Praying that his suspicions were wrong but knowing they were probably right, he walked over and opened the door, looking at the empty bags in the seat that had been filled with money just a few hours before.

"Oh, you son of a..." Mike said, trailing off before he could complete the curse, for it was in that moment that a massive car he recognized pulling into the lot and stopped in front of the hotel office.

Robert stepped out of the car and stared at Mike from across the way. Mike could just make out the smile on his face, and he instinctively went for the spare gun in the glove box of the truck.

"Hold up Mike," Robert said, raising a hand. He took a step away from the car and pulled his phone from out of his pocket, holding it up for Mike to see. "I will call for back-up so that we can mediate this. After all the years in which we've shared business together, I don't see why you have to go for a gun straight away."

Mike relented, pulling away from the truck and standing to face his former boss. "I woke up to a mess on my hands this morning. Not sure that I can trust anyone this late in the game."

"You can still trust me," Robert said. He took another couple of steps towards Mike, both hands up in the air and one of them still cradling the smartphone. "You could always trust me, and you know that. Have I ever given you reason to worry? Let me call for someone to help us work this whole thing out. How's your head doing by the way?"

"Hurts about the same as a day ago," Mike said, shutting the door as he stepped further away from the vehicle. "I still aim to get myself examined once this is over. That is if I get my hands on Johnny and strangle him for taking off with the money we made yesterday."

"I'm sorry that happened Mike. I really am. I can spot you for the money he took, for old time's sake. How about you come back with me into Richmond? We can work out some stuff at the office, and I can hire you on a floating basis. A man can make a lot of money on a floating basis, more than he would just straight working under me."

You're acting fishy and I don't trust you, Mike thought, though he knew better than to come out and say it. *I don't trust you, and I don't know that I can trust anyone again.*

"I don't want the Syndicate life anymore," Mike said. "I didn't want to do what Johnny and me did yesterday neither. Don't know why I let him talk me into it. The thing with my neighbor yesterday morning had me scared, and I guess I wasn't thinking."

"Just like you didn't think with the imported cars," Robert said.

"Yeah, just. 15 liked I didn't think with that. God, how many times you want me to beg and plead for forgiveness over that?"

"Sorry to bring it up Mike, but it was kind of a big deal. Surely cost me a bit in the short run, though I made it all back quickly enough. That's the kind of thing I don't want from one of my top employees, and you proved yourself to be the best I had before that happened."

Just as Mike was about to respond to that a man walked out of the hotel office, carrying a bottle of Jack Daniels and looking like a fool.

Robert turned around drew his gun, pointing it square

at the bottle. "Consider this a one-step program sir," he said, shooting at the middle of the bottle. The glass shattered, dispensing the alcohol to the ground. Robert raised up the gun and shot the man in the chest, knocking him back into the office and drawing fearful screams from inside the building.

"See Mike," Robert shouted, still looking at where he shot the man down, "I can do things without thinking too. The difference is I'm powerful enough to get away with it. You're not."

Robert was forced to turn back around as the sound of a diesel engine pricked at his ears. He turned around to see Mike backing his truck out of the space and speeding out into the road, making a clean break for it. In another second Mike was gone.

Robert smiled, shaking his head. "I'll catch up to you," he said out loud, to no one in particular. "You can't get too far that I won't catch up to you. That's not how this game works. I'll get you, and I will show you the rules." And with that he walked to his car, dialing some numbers into his phone. He needed to make a call before he got too far ahead of himself.

>>>

Inside the office the manager was screaming bloody murder. "Look at all this mess!" he screamed, eyeing the blood and broken glass. "Grant's gonna kill me—he just repainted in here!"

As he went on screaming and losing patience with the situation, the Good Reverend Bragg was losing consciousness as well as the last grip on his life. As he stared up at the ceiling and held his stomach, he began praying little sheepish prayers.

"I shouldn't have gotten mad with you," he muttered, barely loud enough for anyone to hear. "I shouldn't have fallen into the trap of sin. I allowed my misery to overtake me, and for that I'm sorry. Forgive me Father, forgive me..."

And those were the last words he spoke as he entered into the afterlife, leaving the manager to worry about his problems which had an immediate bearing on this present life.

CH. 16: ELMORE MEETS HIS END

Johnny had just pulled into a spot in front of the county jail in Crewe when his boss called him. He pulled his phone and answered it, groaning when he saw the number flash across the screen. "I just made it to the jail now. Am about to do the job in just a few seconds."

"That's all well and good," Robert said on the other end. "I just wanted to tell you that I met Mike at the motel just now. Things were going decently enough, and near as I could tell he didn't suspect a thing. But then something happened, and Mike ended up slipping away from me. I have an idea that he might try and swing back around to his house, but I can't be sure of that. When you are done at the station I'd like for you to meet me back at the office. I hope to reconnect with Mike and convince him to come back with me, but I can't be sure of that either."

Robert then paused for several moments to take a lengthy breath. Then, after what seemed like an eternity of silence, he asked, "You think you can be done with your task soon?"

"Yeah," Johnny said, groaning, "I'll be done soon enough. Will let you know when I'm on my way." He paused and thought things over for a moment, and then said, "I was wondering if you don't just want for me to spring this guy out you had me come and see. Considering the mess of yesterday I don't think I should be wasting this dude, especially if he's working for us."

"Whether it seems like something you should do or not," Robert said, "it's what I want for you to do. So you had better go on and do it and that's that." Robert's tone stiffened with this last line, coming through like a menace. "We aren't in the business of playing nice with the men who make things difficult for us. I made that mistake once, and I don't plan on making that mistake again anytime soon. And besides it's important for you to realize this guy is nothing. Hell, he's less than nothing. He's so small and insignificant it's almost laughable.

"Now you know what I have for you to do, and I have no reason to get on your back and see that you get it done. Just do it and come back to the Richmond office. I'll be seeing you." And with that Robert hung up, leaving Johnny to the task at hand.

Johnny stowed his phone away and walked the rest of the way up the steps, to the front door of the Crewe police station. He could feel a tinge of discomfort as he opened the door and walked inside; this would be the second time in as many days that Johnny has been around a police building, with the last time ending in a sheriff being shot. The dead sheriff in Chase City factored oddly into the job he had here in Crewe, and the interconnectedness of it all gave Johnny concern as he walked up to the front desk and asked the cop who was there, "Do you have an Elmore Johnson back there? I was sent to deal with him."

The cop at the desk pushed Johnny through to the back without one ounce of scrutiny required by his job description. From there he was led into a conference room, where a couple more cops stepped in and had a talk with Johnny. Johnny leveled with them, revealing the name of the man who had sent him and the reason he was sent. Being that Robert Christopher's reach extended out into

Crewe (just as his reached out into everywhere else that fell under the 434 area code), these men gave no further lip as they brought Elmore into the room and left the two of them alone.

"Make sure you are quick with it," said one of the officers as he closed the door. "Some of us are just now coming off the night shift; we would like to get home and make love to our wives." Then he shut the door all the way, leaving Elmore with his destiny.

Johnny pointed to a chair and urged Elmore to take a seat. "Let's have a talk man to man. We both had a long night, so there's no reason why we shouldn't take a load off and relax for a bit." When Elmore sat down (slowly, eyeing this stranger with suspicion) Johnny smiled and took a seat across from him.

For a few moments the two men sat and looked at each other, checking each other out. The silence seemed to swell up between them, threatening to suffocate them both and leave their bodies to rot. Before that happened Johnny let out a sigh, and said, "The boss tells me you had a little skirmish yesterday. Said you were on the way to deal with a job he gave you when you got stopped for gunning a guy down. Is that correct, or am I leaving something out here?"

Elmore blushed, shaking his head. "Yeah, the thing at the Tastee Freeze was a mistake. But I wasn't working the job—not directly anyway. I was going into Chase City to check on the sheriff."

"What does the Chase City sheriff have to do with your job? The boss gave you a task, to investigate Mike; Sheriff Lieber is just a hillbilly cop in a cow-patch town. He had no bearing on the assignment."

"You must not know," Elmore said, shaking his head again. The smile on his face was extra creepy given his current predicament. "Mister Christopher must not have told you. It's so sad really, that you're that much closer to the boss than I but you weren't even told about it."

"Would you care to share with me what I clearly don't know?" asked Johnny. He started tapping his fingers against the part of his jacket directly covering his gun as he considered the man sitting across from him. "Believe me when I tell you this Elmore: I want to help you. But in order to do that I'm gonna need a little more information to go on."

"Well, ok then," Elmore said, leaning over the table. "I guess I can give you a few facts to go on. How much have you got, because this could take 40 days and 40 nights all by itself." And with that Elmore broke off into his spiel, which all totaled took no more than a good hour from start to finish.

Johnny listened with intent as Elmore told him a tale of a shared history with the boy giant at the orphanage, a history of mutual hate developed between a child and his natural enemy. Elmore shivered with rage as he recounted the fight that had left him humiliated before his peers and stripped him of his honor on the playground.

Robert then went on to give an extensive summary of his education and military service after aging out of the system; he was much more brief as he went over his discharge and eventual salvation at the hands of Mister Christopher, whose guidance had kept him lavish with beer and food.

Finally Elmore started to tear up as he started talking about this recent task given him by the boss, the one that had brought the freak of nature back into his life so that he can exact his revenge.

"It was a sure-fire sign sent from God himself," Elmore said, taking a breath. "The Lord Almighty has given me a chance to send that sorry soul straight into the pit of hell."

Johnny glanced at his wristwatch as Elmore gave this last statement with an angry flourish. "That was certainly a situation you have there, my friend. Still leaves the question of what all this has to do with the sheriff of Chase

City. You haven't explained that one to me yet."

Elmore rose up from his chair and started pacing the floor. Sweat was rolling off the back of his neck and soaking the edge of his collar. He moved back and forth on the space between his chair and the outer wall, not looking up from his shuffling feet for several minutes. After a while he started muttering to himself—he wasn't saying any words so much as making low whispery sounds. Doing all of this had the cumulative effect of creeping Johnny out to no end.

"Elmore," Johnny said, clearing his throat, "I am really going to need for you to tell me something here. The sooner we can get through this, the better."

This gentle but forceful prompting on Johnny's part jolted Elmore back into reality. He turned and smiled as he made his way back and settled down into his seat. "I am sorry," he said, shrugging. "I guess that I should go ahead and mention the fact that Sheriff Lieber is actually Michael Liebowitz' father."

Johnny did well at masking his surprise from Elmore's view, though the revelation regarding his partner's parentage certainly did him in for a shock. "Ok, so now I understand. You got it into your head that killing Mike's long lost father could then be used to lord over your childhood enemy as a sort of mental torture. I have to admit it to you, that would have been a wonderful plan. Had you not allowed yourself to do what you did yesterday you would've been able to follow through with it. As it now stands you are simply a liability to the boss."

Elmore perked up at this last bit, as a frown began to appear on his lips. "Did Mister Christopher say that I was a liability? Can I have a chance to explain myself to him? I swear that I can fix all this, I swear that with just a little work it can all be erased—"

"We will be fixing it all right here and now," Johnny said, rising from his seat. He smiled as he pulled out his gun and pointed it at Elmore. "Mister Christopher sent me to handle your mess by taking you out directly. He also said for me to tell you that Sheriff Lieber is dead. You wouldn't have been able to make good on your plan even if you hadn't screwed up and landed yourself in jail."

Elmore seemed more concerned with the news regarding Lieber than he was with the gun currently pointed on him. "The sheriff...is dead?" he asked after a pause, his lips quivering as he started to whimper.

"He is as dead as you are about to be," Johnny said. "You wanna know the interesting part? I happen to have been there when he died yesterday. Would you like to know who killed him? It was the freak you hate so much, good ole Mike Liebowitz. He was my partner, and he managed to do the deed in a span of a second."

Johnny unloaded a string of lead into Elmore's chest before he could even respond to the news in any meaningful way. Blood splattered against the section of wall directly behind where Elmore sat as the bullets passed through his body. As he went on shooting him (until the cartridge holding the bullets ran out) Johnny could feel a rush of adrenalin rushing through his body, filling him with a calming sense of euphoria.

Having now completed his task, Johnny holstered his gun and stepped out of the room to speak with the cops. "Mister Christopher thanks you all for allowing me to come in and do what had to be done. He will be sure to show his gratitude to you later in person." He shook their hands and made his way out of the building, leaving Elmore's body to the police for cleanup, along with the fresh blood on the walls.

Johnny cut across the street from the station, making a point to ignore the stolen car he took to get here. He'd seen a Jeep Wrangler on the way in that he liked the look of, and once he found it in the parking lot of the bank across the way he took just a little bit of work to hotwire it and drive off in relative style.

The destination from Crewe was back at the office, and that was just a few hours' drive into Richmond if he didn't gun it. Johnny figured he would have some questions to ask his boss—chances were that there will be a bit of a disagreement between the two of them—but Johnny was learning to be ok with the concept of going against the man in charge. He figured he would just waltz in and surprise the man with his presence, instead of calling him to forewarn that he was coming, or that he'd finished the job. Right now it was just a blessing to be driving a fairly new model Wrangler, with the silver paint job and the hard top, plus the 4WD, towing package, and a good radio to blare out music that he wanted to listen to for a change.

Maybe I'll get some food at a McDonald's, Johnny thought to himself. But then he had a thought and cursed himself as he turned the Wrangler back around to get back to the station, because he just remembered that he forgot to get the bags of money he left in the Ford sedan.

Ok, so maybe I'll get some extra food from the McDonald's for the aggravation, Johnny thought as he collected the money and turned back to head for Richmond. *The way my luck is going something else is gonna mess up shortly. God almighty—can a day get any worse for a man?*

CH. 17: A SLIGHT DETOUR

It took Robert an extra hour or two to make it to Mike's house, largely because he was taking his own sweet time in getting there. He was in no hurry to find Mike, and besides there was still the off chance that he wasn't at his house so Robert figured he had better curb his expectations just in case.

Blasting jazz music through the car stereo, falling into a rare form of road hypnosis that only seemed to bolster his driving ability rather than inhibit it, Robert was nonetheless struggling to maintain his head. Mike was evermore consuming his time, and even for the peacefulness created by the music playing Robert couldn't help but to repeat the same series of thoughts over and over again: *What in God's name did I ever see in him? What has he ever truly done for me? Am I going crazy? Is my empire going to crumble in Mike's wake?*

But there wasn't an answer, just like any other time the surge of questions popped into his head. Robert Christopher was left with an insatiable inquisitive streak, but there was no way in which to feed it. Which left a man no other choice but to suffer with it till his dying day.

Thus encumbered by random thoughts hijacking his own mind, Robert pulled into a truck stop on the left side of the road and parked in a spot directly in front of the entrance. He got out of the car and walked inside, heading for the coolers along the back wall. He opened one of the sliding glass doors and grabbed a couple bottles of 7-Up, a drink he hasn't had in nearly a decade. Carrying the bottles by their tops with one hand, Robert walked up the center aisle and inspected the various flavors of bagged chips, opting for a bag of classic barbeque. Usually a stickler for calorie content, he took a moment to inspect the ingredients and nutritional information on the back label of the bag. He thought it over for a few moments, and then decided to chance it and buy the chips as well as a few packages of candy.

This small, random shopping spree suddenly hit Robert, and for a brief moment in the day a speck of happiness had been possessed and fully realized. This was a moment which was sorely needed, for it was soon to transcend all the pent up frustration and rage festering inside of Robert's quickly aging body.

For this one moment Robert almost forgot that he was on a wild goose chase, searching for a man he both loved and hated—a man who helped in part to build up the Christopher Crime Syndicate only to try and tear it down in an instant. That man, Michael Liebowitz—who for a time seemed to exist only to exasperate his boss' morality, who then became no more than a fleeting thought exiting the mind, leaving room for bigger and better things.

The happiness seemed to erase everything. No more did Robert feel like his world was in the brink of extinction; no more did he wish for death to take away the drunken nights spent staving off sleep and rest. In the here and now Robert Christopher knew peace, and he knew it well enough to refer to it like he would a favorite lover.

All of this from simply grabbing some snack items from the local truck stop.

Robert walked up to the counter and paid for his

things, smiling like a child as the woman made his change and sent him on his way. He walked out the door and to the car, unlocking the driver side door and reaching over to set the bag of junk food in the passenger seat. Underneath the seat was a spare handgun; the cartridges were stowed in the glove compartment, freshly refilled with bullets.

"Hey Robert! Is that you?" called a voice from across the parking lot. Robert looked up to find Carey Wyatt, a man with a syndicate of his own down in Florida who has a few ties in Virginia.

"Why yes, it is you!" he shouted joyously. "How've you been old friend? I haven't seen you in years!"

Robert plastered on a smile as he took Carey's hand and shook it. "Hey there Carey, how've you been? You're pretty far out from your base kid. Wasn't expecting to see you without having to come down to your state and search you out."

"Yeah," Carey started, laughing, "well you haven't quite blocked me out of every business venture in Virginia yet. I'm handling the exotic pets thing now, hitting up all the major ports along the eastern seaboard. I only drove up here on my way to Newport News to see about some Bornean orangutans that some wealthy foreign nationals wanted me to get for them. Supposed to net me a few million at the top of the quarter. Now that I've got you here I can try and convince you to buy into a piece of the pie. Would be nice to have a friend in Virginia I could trust to hold things up. You could certainly put my Floridian mind at ease."

Robert gritted his teeth, thinking some rather horrid thoughts. Carey Wyatt had always been the shill among his fellow syndicate bosses, going for all the pipe dreams and quick-sinks that make organized crime look like the joke it's painted up to be in those poorly written thriller novels. That it only took him a few seconds in seeing him in order to jump into his pitch made Carey seem all the more cheap and stupid. He would have to be extra slick just to pull himself out from this one and carry on with the rest of his day.

"That sounds like a good deal you have going," Said Robert, backing against his car. "I am afraid I only deal in car and drug imports at the moment, with a little in fixed elections at the local and state level. Last time I tried to get into the animal business it was nothing but a pain for me— I only made fifty percent on the back end, and that's just not enough to hold my interest."

So you're still dealing cars," Carey said. He smiled his stupid, oblivious smile as he spoke, and not for the first time since knowing him Robert had wondered how this insipid excuse for a man managed to build up an empire of his own. Some men seem to have all the luck—or at least enough luck to mock the men who put in the work to get where they are.

"Yeah," Robert responded, chuckling with a slight tinge of discomfort. "I've actually doubled my car operation since I last saw you. Though I must admit to having a tough go at it here lately. No doubt I'm sure you heard of the trouble we had with one of our more recent shipments. I'm actually on my way back from an engagement to deal with the man responsible for that and other recent complications to my ongoing operation."

"You're trying to clean up the messes that Big Mike's made," Carey said, shaking his head. "I heard about that situation—yeah I did. You know, I could've told you that guy was trouble when you first hired him from out of the military. That man is a danger, a walking-talking time bomb. I took one look at him a few years ago when you introduced me, and I wanted to fly back out to the Florida swamp I come from in fear for my life"

"He was better than most of our colleagues gave him credit for at the time," Robert said. "Can still be a great asset if I can get back to him and convince him to reverse his resignation that he handed me a few nights ago. That's why I really have to go now Carey—I'm trying to get a hold of Michael at his house, and I'm still over an hour out of Richmond now."

"I don't want to take up much of your time Robert," Carey said. "It sounds like you have a lot on your plate. I do hope that you would take an hour or two and have a meal with me though. It's been so long since we saw each other, and I would still like to have a chance to try and convince you of this new market I've tapped.

How about it Robert?" Carey continued, taking on a soft whine to his voice. "Let's get a bite to eat, and I'll run through some numbers with you. Mike can hold off till later."

"It's getting a tad late for me," Robert complained, trying to maintain a diplomatic tone. He could feel the moment of peace rapidly slipping from him, and he was ready to lay his fellow man to waste for the crime of taking it away. "I do have to get going if I hope to catch. It was great seeing you though—I hope to gather you and some of the other syndicate heads together soon. Maybe we can head down to Florida and hire a private cruise boat for a party off of the gulf for several days. Does that sound good to you? Ok then, let's keep in touch. Take care Carey."

Robert made to climb back into his car, but Carey grabbed him by the elbow and held him in place. "Come on brother, let's go and get something to eat. It's not often that we get a chance to sit down together and compare notes over cold beer and sandwiches. I need a man like you in the pet trade with me. I am afraid I can't take no for an answer—we run the risk of losing a lot of money on the back end, and I could use the extra investment and confidence from you to pull us through to the next quarter. Please Robert, I need for you to help me. As a brother in the order, you are obligated."

As a brother in the order, you are obligated.

A flicker of anger flickered across Robert's eyes when Carey grabbed his arm. Any touch of calm now completely gone, replaced by an ever-growing kernel of rage. After easing himself from his grip, Robert put on a smile and said to Carey, "Ok brother, you got it. I'll be glad to have you for lunch. There are a few diners up ahead from here; all you have to do is pick one and we'll eat there. I'll even drive you in my car."

Carey all too excitedly agreed to that and walked around to the passenger side of the car. Robert got in on the driver side and cleared the stuff out of the passenger seat, setting it in the back. They both settled in their seats and slammed their doors shut in unison; it was like a perfectly calibrated machine in the way they synchronized these little movements. Robert put his key in the ignition and started the car, backing out into the road without even bothering to look out for any cars that might be coming along.

Robert drove in silence as Carey talked his ear off, allowing for one violent thought flow into another as the man to his right pushed him further into the deep end with his utter lack of awareness. With no one else on the road at that precise moment, with the outside world passing them by in the rear window, Robert couldn't help but to relish in the warm glow of satisfaction as the crime he was planning at this very moment would be seen by no one else other than God himself.

And Robert didn't care if the Lord Almighty did bear witness to his handiwork.

Carey looked out the window and immediately pointed to a sign for a restaurant that was up ahead. "We can go there and eat. I'm not picky, none at all. Just a good sandwich and plenty of coffee before I even touch a beer, and I feel content. How does that sound to you Robert?"

Robert didn't even give the sign a moment's notice as he passed right on by.

"Hey Robert," Carey asked, "did you hear what I said about that place back there? It looked perfect to me, though if you know of a place that's better I'm down. I'm really not picky at all."

"You ever read any of the novels by Jim Thompson?" Robert asked, his eyes focused on the road immediately ahead of him.

"No," Carey said, beginning to tense in his seat. "No sir, I can't say that I have."

"I gave Mike some of my old paperbacks when he quit from me the other night," Robert said. "One of them was this gem titled *The Killer Inside Me*. It features this deputy sheriff by the name of Lou Ford, who seems to everybody in town as cordial and just a tad on the simple side. In reality he's a cold, calculating killer and sadomasochist, and one of the things he likes doing is goading people into frustration with an endless stream of clichés and meaningless platitudes. I was thinking just now that you remind me a lot of ole Lou, except that you aren't half as smart as he is."

"Listen man," Carey said. "I don't mean to hassle you about the pet thing. I'm sorry for going heavy on the pitch, and I promise I won't bring it up anymore if you don't want me to."

"I'm not upset," Robert said, turning into a side road that was densely populated with large oak trees on either side. "Least I'm not as upset as I was at the top of our conversation today. Tell you the truth I feel fine, and I suspect in another minute you'll feel fine too. Least I hope you'll feel fine, though I reckon I wouldn't have a way of checking on you to see how you'll feel. I have no connection with the afterlife, though I guess I could find a priest who can give me some words of advice after I'm done with you."

Robert laughed at his own nonsense, and continued to laugh as he parked the car in a secluded spot and led Carey out in the woods to kill him. By the time he walked back to his car he'd stopped, the overwhelming sense of peace and happiness starting to return back to him. He got in the car and drove back out on the main road, and made his way to Richmond to see about another man who'd been cause for frustration to him, but in this case Robert felt no need to let the frustration consume him. For he was a man with zen-like wisdom, and should he finish with his tasks in time he would set out to spread his wisdom to all the world.

So long as Mike turned up when he made it into Richmond.

CH. 18: RELOCATING

Mike took his sweet time driving into Virginia Beach, largely because he had to stop a few times along the way to rob a few fast food restaurants and a couple of gas stations. Seeing as Johnny took off with most of the money (save for a small bankroll that he'd shaved off for emergencies such as the one he was in now), there wasn't a choice but to run a couple of quick jobs to make up the difference. This served to push Mike's anger levels beyond acceptable levels, so he had to kill some people at the last couple of places he robbed. It was nothing personal—some people just happen to be at the wrong place at the wrong time.

It wasn't until he neared the campus of Regent University that Mike started to feel just a little guilty for what he'd done. He wasn't sorry for the money he took; that was nothing more than a man working his skills and making a respectable living. But the casual shooting down of civilians was starting to weigh down on Mike, and Mike didn't like to have things weighing down on him. He would have to find a nearby place to hunker down and clear his head for a minute, but he didn't want it to be near a religious school. He was afraid the conscience of Pat Robertson would haunt him, and he didn't care to have that kind of supernatural element coming out of the woodwork.

Cutting through random streets until he reached Providence Road, Mike turned into the parking lot of a strip mall that housed, among other things, a store whose sign read SMITH'S DISCOUNT BOOKS AND CIGARETTES. Mike smiled as he parked and walked up to the storefront.

Mike hadn't smoked but once his entire life, but with the way his nerves were jittering about under his skin he figured he would probably need to pick them up again. More importantly, there was the real adventure in walking through a dingy hole-in-the-wall bookstore, the kind of adventure most people that Mike knew would have never gone on (especially his fellow members of the criminal fraternity). The smell of pages covered with ink was just too good to pass up; a man needed very much to find that smell, and have a few moments of time to unwind as the world burns outside.

And thus hoping to hide out for a little while before he had to find lodging for the night, Mike walked into the store and caught sight of the older, heavyset proprietor manning the counter.

"Well aren't you a big fella," said the old man. "I don't see too many walk in here as big as you. Course there aren't a lot to walk in here at all these days. Currently in a down season and I lost both my workers due to them moving away to Florida." The old man shook his head. "I don't know why I'm telling you all this, being as I don't know you from dirt. Guess you have one of those honest faces that makes it easy to trust you instantly."

Mike smiled awkwardly. "You have any Donald Westlake? A friend gave me some Thompsons, but I guess I'm more in the mood for more lighthearted capers than books that feature psychopathic men and hard-spirited women."

"I think I just got a few Westlakes in trade last week," the old man said, pointing down the middle aisle. "They'd be down that aisle there, with the other mysteries."

Mike thanked the man and went down the aisle till he found the books filed under "W." He scanned the titles for a minute before picking up what looked to be a recent reprint of Westlake's own *The Hot Rock*. Mike could vaguely remember reading this one during his last year at the orphanage; his favorite teacher, Mister Carter, had given him a stack of Dortmunder novels, and Mike read all of them three or four times. Those were among the best memories Mike ever had of the place, though thinking of brought chills, along with a tinge of sadness. Mike frowned as he considered Carter, a man with whom he'd kept in touch during his stint in the military. He hadn't talked with the man since going into a seedier line of work, though he did still think of him every so often.

Looking at the cover of the book in his hand, Mike wondered what would happen if he looked his old teacher up and talked with him—would the man know the stains that now marked his soul? If he did, would he still care about him?

Mike did his best to push these thoughts out from of his mind as he carried the book up to the counter, placing it before the old man at the counter. "I'll be buying this from you today. Saw a sign that read fifty-percent off; does that include this one?"

The old man smiled as he picked up the book and handed it to Mike. "Why don't you just take it, and accept an act of kindness from me. You look like you could use a little kindness your way to counteract some very bad luck."

Mike took the book, giving the man a look. " Well, I appreciate certainly it." Then he had a thought and said, "You said you were down some workers. Think you could stomach the cost for hiring someone new? I never worked in a bookstore before, but I know my way around one from being in plenty of them as a customer. Could use the time to ground myself to the town while I look around some."

"Oh are you new to the area?" The old man asked.

"Just rolled in this morning.," Mike said. "I'll be looking for a place to stay once I leave from here."

"There's a couple of cheap hotels down the road to hold you over. There's a realter just a couple doors down that can hook you up with an apartment somewhere. Might need more than what I can pay you to cover rent and food."

"I have a private source of income that can cover my expenses," Mike answered grimly. "I want the experience more than anything."

"Sure, experience is a wonderful thing." The old man thought a moment, and then rose from his stool behind the counter and reached out his hand for Mike to shake. "The name's Thomas Smith. I'm your new boss I reckon. Welcome to have you aboard. I still have a couple hours before I technically close, but what's say I end the day early and we grab dinner and get to know each other better?"

"I'm Michael Liebowitz. That sounds good to me—I've been hungering for a good mom and pop pizza. Oops!—one second if you don't mind. I think I feel my phone vibrating." Mike pulled out his cell and saw Johnny's name flash across the screen, Shaking his head, he declined the call and put the phone back into his pocket.

"It was somebody I don't feel like talking with." Mike said apologetically. "I can just call him back."

"I get enough calls like that to make me wanna shoot the inventor of telephones," said Thomas. "Let's go on out of here. Got an excellent Italian place on the other side of the strip. I'll walk you down there if you don't mind the exercise."

"Lead the way," Mike said. He watched as the old man walked around the counter, and then followed as he turned off all the lights and walked out the door to lock up. As he stood out in the sidewalk he gave a brief thought to Johnny calling him, feeling a tad worried even though he knew he should be boiling over with rage over the situation from earlier.

125

He must be in trouble if he's going to call me knowing I'd likely chew him out, Mike thought. *I wonder what he could wan. Whatever it is, I hope he knows well enough to expect a world of hurt when I call him back later. He and Robert both had better know well enough to keep their distance from me until I figure this all out.*

Mike quickly brushed these thoughts aside as Thomas tapped him on the shoulder and led him down the sidewalk, telling him all the virtues of the little Italian eatery they were about to enjoy.

"I eat at least one meal a day at this place," Thomas said with a chuckle. "Sometimes I take in two meals in a day. They all know me by name, and the cook's wife flirts with me I swear. Their daughter might be around your age—which is strange for me to say, since I don't know how old you are. In any case, you're going to have a time at this place. I can guarantee it."

CH. 19: MAKING AMENDS

Johnny knew he risked drawing his boss' ire for not calling him after killing Elmore, and he also knew that calling Mike could potentially draw a rage as of yet unseen by anyone on earth. That was of course dependent on whether Mike would pick up the phone and answer him when he called; so far he's let all ten calls go to voicemail.

Catching Mike's voicemail greeting for the twelfth time, Johnny cursed himself again and listened through the whole thing, waiting to get to the end so that he could leave a message:

This is Mike Liebowitz. I can't come to the phone right now, but leave a name and number and I will get back with you as soon as possible. If you're a woman I went on a recent date with, looking for a reconnection, I am willing to negotiate. If you're my long-lost mother seeking to look through my banking statements, you won't get a red cent until you go through a DNA test. Thank you, and have a good day. Click.

Knowing finally that he wasn't getting anywhere, Johnny hung up and tossed his phone into the passenger seat of the Wrangler as he drove into the same garage where he met Mike the other day to change out his plates and have a quick paint job. He would have to do these things if he wanted to keep his new ride, along with a fix on the wires he tore out to hotwire the thing, plus a new set of keys and some doctored paperwork just in case he were to ever get pulled over. With most of the boys in blue being on the payroll, the paperwork was nothing more than a formality—but Johnny had run enough risks as it was, and he wanted to start playing it safe again.

Over the past couple of days Johnny's whole person had undertaken multiple severe changes—a steady back-and-forth between one thing and another that had begun taking its toll on his psyche. Johnny certainly didn't like what he was becoming, but he couldn't think of a good way in which to stop it.

Johnny wondered how much of it had to do with his partner...

...or rather his ex-partner.

Johnny had never understood the full nature of the dynamic between him and Mike. From the start of their working relationship there had been a friendly spark, the kind of spark one feels ignited only once in a lifetime. It was the sort of thing that happens only when you encounter the one who you know immediately as your best friend for life. When you find such a friend and realize it, you can only understand how much it hurts to have them turn away after something comes along to wreck everything. By then it can be too late to do a thing about it.

Johnny hoped that it wasn't too late. He prayed to any god that would listen to make it so it wasn't too late—with every successive call he placed, and every minute spent waiting in the garage for them to fix up his new ride, Johnny could feel the glimmer of hope rise and fall with the tide of rampant thoughts running through his head. Chief among those thoughts was the fact that maybe, just maybe, it really was too late; a man had to be equally prepared to receive the bad as well as the good, so he wouldn't be disappointed in either case.

"Hey Johnny," called the head mechanic. "we got a call for you on the line in the office. It's the boss. Says you haven't been answering your cell. He sounds pretty pissed."

Johnny rolled his eyes as he made his way to the office and took the phone. He took the receiver to his ear and said, "Sorry boss—I meant to call you and just forgot. But I did the job, so it's no problem."

"It's a problem if I say it's a problem," Robert said coldly. "It's a mighty big problem too. I can't have you neglecting to check in with me on a regular basis. Something could go wrong and I'd be out of the loop—for a boss being out of the loop is as close to killing me off as anything. You might as well send me to the incinerator to dance with the flames, because I'm dying!"

"All I did was forget to call right away and tell you that I killed the guy off," Johnny scoffed. "Nothing's going down in flames. You're not dying."

"I'm the one who oversees the books Johnny," Robert scolded. "I don't remember you pouring over the job reports at all hours of the night, worrying over every detail and wondering where the next disaster is going to come from. Until you take over and do for the company what I've been doing—until you put in your blood, sweat and tears—why don't you just leave the damage assessment to me. Is that good, is that ok with you?"

"Yeah," Johnny said, motioning for the mechanic to leave the office. "That's ok with me. Is there anything else you needed? Do you still want for me to meet you at the office? I shouldn't be long where I'm at; I just needed to change out some parts on this new car I got."

There was a long pause on the other end of the line. Johnny waited to see whether his boss was going to say anything, and when no words came forth he asked, "You still there boss?"

Finally Robert responded. "Tell me you didn't steal a car. Tell me you didn't do it Johnny."

"All right, so then I guess I won't tell you."

Robert growled so loud on the other end that Johnny had to pull the phone away from his head to keep from shattering his eardrum. "You no-good sorry excuse for a man! Who do you think you are? We're running the risk of losing everything but the shirts off our backs, and you're gonna go and steal a car? What kind of car did you even rip off?"

"It's just a Jeep Wrangler boss."

"So lemme get this straight," Robert said, lowering his tone to a more adequate level but still gritting his teeth and shoving them through the enamel with his tongue. "You decide to steal a car, after killing a man in jail and without so much as bothering to call me and let me know anything, and you steal a junkpile on wheels like a frigging Jeep Wrangler. Is that what you're telling me?"

"That's what I'm telling you," Johnny said. He felt the sting of having his Jeep referred to as a junkpile, but he chose not to say anything about it.

"Unbelievable. Simply unbelievable. I tell you what you're gonna do: you're gonna meet me in my office, just as soon as you quit playing matchbox cars at the garage. You're gonna meet with me, and we're going to put our heads together and figure out what were gonna do about Mike. Do you understand what I'm saying to you?"

"Yes Mister Christopher. I understand what you're saying to me."

"Say that to me again. Say it slower, so I know the words are sinking into you."

Sinking into me? Is he serious? "I understand what you're saying to me," Johnny said, drawing out every syllable until it took him half a minute to get the sentence out of his mouth.

"Ok, good. Now hurry it along and get down to my office. I have to make a quick stop before I make it back anyway, so you have a little time before you have to meet with me.

And Johnny?" Robert continued. "Don't make any stupid decisions in the meantime. Thanks."

Click.

Johnny put the receiver back down and walked out of the office. He called out to one of the mechanics working on the Jeep. "You mind if I get my cell from out of there?"

"Here, I'll get it." The guy walked around from the front of the car and opened the passenger door, reaching in and grabbing the phone. He closed the door and brought the phone over to Johnny. "Here you go man. We should only be a little longer on this one. We would've gone faster, but Rick loves the new Jeeps and he just had to go over everything with a fine-tooth comb."

"No problem," Johnny said. "Thank you so much." He took his cell and walked out of the garage, dialing the number to Mike's phone again. He listened to it ring until he got the voicemail again. This time he decided to leave a message:

"Hey Mike, it's me. Look, I know you probably have a lot of questions. You're probably even too pissed to wanna hear my answers right now. What I did was ridiculous, and I feel pretty bad about it. We go a long way together, and I would hope that time alone would warrant me the chance to try and make things right again. Just...uh...please, just call me back so we can talk about this. I'll talk to you later man."

Click.

Johnny slid the phone back into his pocket and started pacing around in front of the garage door. A million thoughts were running through his head, most of them being possible ways of procuring a peace offering for Mike. Everything had gone about a hundred different shades of bad in the course of a couple days, and the life that Johnny thought he knew didn't seem to make sense anymore. Even if he could make it right with Mike—and that would be a pretty big *if*—there was still a lot of mess to clean up, and it could take a while to even begin a job that big.

And then in the middle of all of that Johnny had another thought, this one concerning his boss. The man demanded that he come to the office as soon as possible, and yet had made it seem like it might take him a while to get there himself. The boss-man was starting to change his demeanor and person as well—no more was the steady and collected hand that had guided the whole operation, for that had suddenly been replaced with a hand that shook with rage and paranoia. Something was going on with the head of the Syndicate, and Johnny hadn't a clue as to what that thing could be.

Whatever it was, it was sure to be a threat to everything.

CH. 20: MIKE'S NEW ROUTINE

Over a couple slices of meat lover's pizza apiece Thomas worked over the details of Mike's upcoming employment at his store. "I'm afraid I can't do much more than three days a week to start. We get some more business to come in and I maybe can add another day or two. Most everyone comes in now only want to buy a pack of Camels or Newports and then turn round and leave. I can't seem to get any overlap between the smokers and the readers."

Mike nodded as he laid his half-eaten slice on his plate. "I might have a few ideas for how you can advertise," he said, diverting his eyes between the plate and his new boss. "We don't even have to blow a lot of money. Can do this whole grass-roots sort of thing in the immediate area and double the foot traffic. Triple even."

Thomas looked at Mike with wide-eyed wonder. "My god," he said. "I wonder how a man gets to know so much about business and marketing."

"It comes from watching a lot of *Shark Tank* in my free time," Mike said. "Picked up all kinds of juicy business tips. Never had a chance to use any of them till now. My former boss didn't exactly employ me for my marketing skills." As he said this last part Mike began to chuckle uncomfortably, his cheeks reddening.

"Your former boss sounds like an incompetent little fruitcake," said Thomas. He let out a good-hearted laugh and shook his head. "Sorry, I know I shouldn't say that. You do sound like you've a story though, concerning your boss. Not sure if you'd be down to share it at some point. I'd be down to listen—if and when you're ready of course."

"I may take you up on your offer and bend your ear a bit," said Mike, picking his slice back up. "Not sure that I feel up for it today, or for the next little while. I like you just fine from just meeting you, but I'd like for us to get better acquainted before I divulge personal details like that."

"All right," Thomas said, "that's fine with me kid." He went ahead and grabbed another slice for himself and continued talking. "I got to respect a man who doesn't give up so much all at once. The store's awful quiet most days, with lots of time for reading and conversation. You can talk to me about most anything throughout the day. When you're not reading Westlake that is."

He gave Mark a little wink as he said this last part, looking rather fatherly as he did so. A second later he bit into the new slice, groaning happily.

As Mark was just starting to feel himself being charmed by this older gentleman's mannerisms, he also felt a lingering sense of confusion and regret over just how quickly everything was moving before him. Was he really ready to jump into the drudgery of low-wage work and living generally hand to mouth? Mike had to admit that the change in pace was somewhat tempting; the question was what to do with his savings and house, neither of which should remain under the name Michael Liebowitz.

I will to have to play it safe juggling everything for the next while, Mike thought to himself.

It was at that moment that Mike felt his phone vibrate in his pocket. He pulled it out just as it went to voicemail, and saw on the screen that he'd received a bunch of missed calls and several voicemails from Johnny Gunn—the best friend turned traitor. Mike showed no emotion as he took the phone in both hands and crushed it into a few dozen pieces of plastic and circuit board over the table. He dropped the mauled mess next to his plate, and only after inspecting his handiwork did Mike crack a humorous smile.

"Now why would you do a dumb thing like that?" asked Thomas, completely dumbfounded. He dropped the crust of his pizza onto his plate, having devoured the last of its more succulent offerings the moment before.

Mike shrugged simply, the expression on his face still lacking in emotion. "Guess I was just itching to go out and buy a new phone." What Mike didn't tell him—what he couldn't tell him—was that it had only just occurred to him that the cell was a prime conduit for Mister Christopher or the untainted members of the cop fraternity to lock in on his whereabouts. The gross incompetence of these people (as Mike was also starting to see) didn't do much to calm the man's worry, for he knew that even the dumbest of the dumb could very well luck into something that would then be used against him.

I'm going to need to be extra careful when handling my savings and affairs, Mike thought to himself. *And how do I go about dealing with my house? The neighbors are more than likely clamoring for my head as it stands, and I'm sure that abandoning the place will only raise a few more red flags right along with what I did to the bastard living next door from me.*

"What's going through that big head of yours?" Thomas asked, jolting Mike awake. He sat there looking into his new employee's eyes, as though desperately searching for whatever secrets could be found therein. "You aren't having second thoughts about working for me are you? Or maybe some doubts you dare not say out loud?"

Mike shook his head. "Nah, nothing like that. I just got some old dreams that don't wanna quit on me just yet. I'm sure you know how that is. They'll vacate the premises on their own time; it's just a matter of playing the waiting game."

Thomas laughed, though there was a certain lack of conviction in his voice that suggested he still felt uncomfortable from the phone thing just moments before. "You certainly are an odd duck Mike. I can't quite put my finger on you—I swear you're up to something, though what that something is I haven't a clue. You seem decent enough though." Then he chuckled, snorted, and added, "Hell, I doubt you did anything as bad as say...well, as bad as killing anybody."

Thomas laughed riotously over his own little joke, not noticing how that Mike had begun shifting uncomfortably in his seat.

Finally Thomas calmed down enough to ask Mike, "So what is it that you aim to do in the long term?" He started looking around anxiously for the waitress as he grabbed at the leftover pizza. "Hold that thought for a minute will? Hey miss—can I get a to go box for these last few slices? Thank you." The young woman nodded and went to get the box; satisfied for the moment, Thomas shifted his attention back on Mike. "Now what was I saying? Oh yes, what are your plans for the evening? I don't know if that was exactly the question, but it was close enough."

"Well," Mike said, leaning forward in his seat. "I reckon the first thing I'll do is find a temporary place to stay while searching through the apartment ads. Then I guess I could head over to a Walmart and get a few days' worth of cheap clothes. I'm rolling into town with only an extra day's worth of slacks and skivvies, so I'm basically starting over from scratch."

"Sure," Thomas said, the good humor draining further from his cheeks. "Well that certainly sounds like a plan to me." His eyes began to divert away to the walls of the restaurant, never quite reaching Mike for any length of time. Mike could sense that he was beginning to lose the man just a tad; he would have to start winning him back in short order.

"I guess I should find a place to meet other interesting people," Mike said finally, after taking a few moments to try and think of something—anything—which would pull him out of the hole he'd dug himself into. "Been largely by myself in the loving department for a bit, if you know what I mean. I could go for a girl who would go steady with me pretty regular."

"Oh!" Thomas shouted, with a surge of cheerful excitement. "I know exactly what you should do." He jumped from his seat just as the waitress came over with the box, nearly smacking into her. "Oops.' he said to her, blushing. "I am awful sorry for jumping at you like that." He took the box from her and sat back down; when the waitress left he turned back to Mike and said in a hushed voice, "As I was gonna say, you should go and find a good church nearby. If you wanna meet a girl you need to meet her at a Sunday service. Was how I met my first two wives...as well as the forty-something I'm seeing now."

He gave Mike a knowing wink as he said this last part, causing the new employee to feel just a tad guilty. Then he laughed as he stowed the leftover pizza into the box. "I hope you don't want any more of this," he said. "I might feel a second dinner coming along later on tonight when I catch the 11 o'clock local news."

"I'm good," Mike said, waving the pizza off. He and Thomas made an agreement to meet up at the front of the store first thing in the morning so that they can go over the ways of bookselling (along with a bit on the smoke trade thrown in for good measure). Once they'd worked out the particulars Thomas went up to the front and paid the check, and Mike followed him out the door toward the lot where Mike had left his truck.

"That's a nice truck you have there," Thomas said, as they reached the tailgate of Mike's vehicle. "Looks like you had a paint job fairly recently."

"Yeah," Mike said, "I'm starting to regret that now." He started circling around the truck and inspected the uneven lines with vigor. "The guys I used usually do good work, but I was in a mad crunch for time when I had them do the job and they rushed it more than they should have. I guess I'll just have to suffer it in leisure." Mike let off a chuckle as he went around to the driver side and opened the door, reaching over to place his newly bought paperback in the passenger seat.

"That's a shame," Thomas said. "I hope you can find some new people to do your work for you now that you're in the 7-5-7 area." He grinned as he shook Mike's hand. "Now you go on and consider what I told you—get up off your hind end and visit some of these churches around here. You might find something worth keeping here and setting down roots. While I think of it, why don't you hit up Norfolk sometime and catch a movie at the Naro theater. They're very arthouse in their movie selection, but I like them just fine."

"I'll be sure to check them out," Mike said. "Thanks for the suggestion." He said goodbye and climbed into his truck, cranking the engine with the key as he shut the door behind him. He quickly adjusted the radio until he landed on a political-talk AM station, and then when he felt ready he pulled out of the lot. At that moment Mike figured he would take up Thomas' suggestion and check out some of the local churches—with a couple of small detours along the way. A man had to think about fattening his wallet pretty quick if he wanted to stay in town for any length of time.

Mike toured the parking lot of every church along Providence road, and was genuinely surprised at how much he liked looking at all the buildings. Never having much use for the finer points of architecture, he nonetheless could feel himself being drawn to the oversized archways housing massive stained-glass windows depicting scenes such as the Christ dying on the cross for the sins of the world. Seeing the picture in the windows, Mike started to feel a momentary glimmer of guilt for the things he had done and was set on continuing to do. But it was only for a moment, and soon enough it was gone.

After sitting in the parking lot of one of the half dozen Presbyterian churches for the night, Mike decided to go and find an open bar in which to find some capable female company. He figured he could try and seduce someone in the same manner he seduced the young woman in the truck stop; this time he could work his game and not have the pressures of a job to prevent him from sealing the deal. Just thinking about that radiant olive-skinned girl from the truck stop filled Mike with that old familiar hunger, leading him to ask himself whether he should go and try to look that little waitress up sometime.

What could it hurt?

Pushing these thoughts off to the side for the time being, Mike drove around till he made it to Independence Boulevard and spotted Kelly's Tavern, located at the end of a strip mall that also had a Walmart. For a moment Mike considered running the clothes errand after the beer-and woman run—the joys of multitasking were self-evident.

Mike pulled into the lot and parked the truck. He shut off the engine and climbed out, taking his sweet time as he walked up to the door and opened it. He could tell just by looking inside that there were plenty of women hanging out in there, drinking and laughing like there was no tomorrow. Just seeing the potential they carried filled Mike's spirit with a newfound joy.

As soon as he sat down at the bar a young redhead in her twenties turned to smile at him. Mike gave her a little wave, and she giggled and quickly turned to her friend sitting next to her. Mike thought that she was cute, but figured her to be a little immature in her young age—he was looking for someone a little more on his level tonight.

After a good twenty minutes—in which time Mike drank several beers—an auburn-haired woman who looked closer to Mike's age approached him from the other end of the bar.

"The name's Julia," she said, offering her hand. "Are you new in town? I don't think I've seen you in here before, and I'm pretty good at recognizing faces." Her smile was radiant under the glow of the neon lights; she appeared to Mike as a sexy bar angel, coming to save his soul from the depths of loneliness and despair.

"I'm Michael," Mike said, taking her hand and returning her smile. "Yeah, you probably never saw me in here before. I don't come by this way often. It's actually my first time coming into this bar; I was thinking of a change of scenery for a small party for two, if you knew of anything else that was good to do."

"Oh baby, I know of a place that's good," Julia said, sliding in close next to Mike's stool. She lowered her voice and added, ""Are you any good?"

Mike considered his answer before looking Julia in the eye and saying, "I guess you could say that I'm good at being bad. I'm almost too good, but I haven't had any complaints near as I can tell."

As he said this Mike gave his newfound friend a little wink. She blushed and placed her hand on his knee. "So you're new to the area," she said playfully." Now, see, I take that to mean you don't have a place to stay for the night. Is that correct?"

"I was looking for a room to hold me down till I get a place of my own," Mike said. he leaned into Julia's touch, seeming to engulf her in the shadow of his glare. "Again, it would be nice to have some company in the meantime."

"I'd keep you company for as long as you can stand it," said Julia, her cheeks heavy with the dew of arousal. "I can see we'll have lots of fun together, and I very much like the idea of that."

140

Mike nearly forgot about having to report to the bookstore in the morning; he was half in love with this woman, and it hardly took any time for him to fall. He took one look at Julia as he rose from his stool in order to pay for his tab, and he swore he could feel butterflies.

"I reckon I should go ahead and see about getting your number Hot Stuff," Julia said, sliding her arm into Mike's as he led her out the door. "Will that be ok with you, or is that too soon for now?"

"I'm in the process of switching phone carriers," Mike said. "I had a smart phone but it broke in my hands earlier today. If we go on liking ourselves after tonight you can come with me after work tomorrow to see about a new setup. Then I will see about giving you my number."

CH. 21: SEVERANCE PAY

Johnny drug his feet in getting to the warehouse, and he continued dragging them down the hall toward the office where his boss had wanted to meet with him. There was still so much up in the air that Johnny couldn't know what to expect over the course of this employee-employer evaluation. He'd hoped to get a hold of Mike before going in, but his former partner hadn't so much as texted him back.

To say that Johnny was now concerned for his future would be an understatement.

Johnny reached the office door knocked against the foggy glass. "Come right on in," he heard Robert call from inside. He opened the door and walked in, moving slowly so as to keep from the hinges squeaking too loudly against the doorframe. He then walked up to the desk and stood there, eyeing the chair where Robert sat, turned so that its back was facing him.

"Glad to see you can finally make it back into," Robert said, making no effort to turn around and face his underling. "I shall expect for you to be on call from here on out, with a substantial pay cut—as punishment for your carefree attitude when it comes to keeping me informed. I would expect better from all men under my employ."

This bit of news nearly sent Johnny to his knees. He

was beyond frustrated—he was livid! "I've had my share of crazy hit me up over the last few days," he said, hoping that Robert would turn around finally and face him like a real man. "I have always followed your lead, and done my job to the best of my abilities. In the process I lost a friend and partner, and that's not just something I can forget like talking about it. I would appreciate a little grace here."

Robert spun around in his chair and looked Johnny dead in the eye. "Grace is for church my friend. You want forgiveness and mercy you had better locate your nearest priest. I'm not in the business of making you feel spiritually and mentally redeemed. In fact I won't be in business at all much longer if I don't close some gaps and tie up loose ends."

Johnny felt about ready to jump over the desk and wrap his hands around Robert's neck. He wanted to choke the life out of him, and in the heat of the moment he wished that he could believe in the supernatural—because he wanted to raise his boss back from the dead, just so he can kill him again. This thought gave Johnny's soul a small comfort, but only a small comfort and no more than that.

Robert, oblivious to Johnny's ire, got up from his chair and went for a nearby bottle of vodka. "Would you care for a glass? I would hate to polish this whole thing by myself. Don't get me wrong—I'd love to drain this bottle, but considering what we have to discuss I think it would be best if I keep a clear head."

"Do you think you've kept a clear head?" Johnny asked him. "In the past year, and even since the freak out with the cars, you have been losing your marbles gradually. The whole operation's ready to go caput, and you stand at the helm of your own company's demise. That doesn't seem like clear thinking to me."

"It's a tad early for you to be making accusations against me," Robert said. "Especially since I'm not even done investigating you for your crimes against my business interests. By the end of this you may not have a so much as a leg to stand on—and I long to see the day when I can lay you to rest for all that you and your little buddy have done to my empire."

"Wait," Johnny said. "Now hold up a moment. What are you even talking about? You act like you're ready to drop the ax on me right here and now."

Robert giggled as he opened the bottle of vodka, and he continued giggling as he grabbed a fresh glass in which to pour a drink. Then he chuckled as he filled the glass and set the bottle on the desk. Robert only stopped with the general giddiness for long enough to bring the glass to his lips, ready to take a drink. He stopped to look at Johnny and say, "The only problem is that up to now I've been hesitant on axing you. You ought to thank me for being for being so lax on that. I won't be as merciful after tonight."

Johnny could feel his anger rising within him, threatening to burst from his chest and hit Robert like a lightning bolt. It was all he could do to keep his rage in check as he sat down in one of the chairs in front of the desk, allowing the entirety of his body to deflate as he fell into the cushiony embrace of the seat.

After a few moments' silence Johnny groaned, and said, "What is it that you aim to do boss?"

Robert smiled as he drained the glass and went for a refill. "I aim to do a lot," he said, with a slight slur to his voice as he spoke. "At least I aim to do a lot more for myself than you and Mike have ever done for me."

Johnny let that little jab against him and his former partner go for the moment; he thought it best to hold the anger in check for a while longer, but he figured he was coming close to the point where he would have to unleash his fury against Robert, this office, and the building they were in if necessary.

Robert continued with his drunken tirade. "I visited Mike's house before coming into the office to meet you. Had a little walk-through before coming out and talk with some of the neighbors. They were rather rude to me, just as Carey Wyatt was when I ran into him earlier—"

"You ran into Carey?" Johnny asked. "What's he doing in town? His network's based in Orlando, though I know he's trying to partner up with all the other syndicates."

"That's why he came to Virginia," Robert said, not quite appreciative over being interrupted in this way. "He was looking to buddy up in an effort to get me to finance one of his crummy schemes. I have him a crude veto on that and sent him on his way. His way to rot in hell that is."

Johnny caught on to thinly veiled double-meaning of that last bit, but he chose not to remark on it. As angry as he was, he knew better than to push the envelope just yet.

"In any case," Robert continued, "I had to handle a few people in Mike's neighborhood, and I will have to pay off some court officials to keep the heat off of me for a while. At least for long enough until I can get my sights back on Mike. I had him in the palm of my hand at the hotel—I was this close to having him over and done with—and because of some sorry punk walking up behind me from out of the office I turned my eye from the target and let him slip by me. Now how do you like them apples?"

Robert gave Johnny a look, expecting him to answer.

"I don't care for them apples," Johnny answered, "nor do I care for the way you've shirked your responsibilities."

Robert looked at Johnny wide-eyed. "Oh please," he said. "Do tell."

"You could've punished him after the car incident," Johnny continued. "The night it all went to hell you had the chance. You had a chance every night since to handle the mess. Until now you've allowed everything to slide, and even in taking up the slack you've proven to be behind the curve in enacting your petty revenge. So no, I don't like them apples. I don't like them one bit, and I think you had better pick another bushel before coming into the kitchen looking for an apple pie to be made."

"You have a lot of nerve," Robert said, pouring himself another glass.

"I've the same nerve as you," Johnny retorted. "In fact I'd say you have no business telling me about the nerve I have." He paused a moment, then smirked as he added, "I noticed you never bothered to tell Mike that the sheriff of Chase City was really his father."

Robert gasped, looking Johnny dead in the eye. He had the bottle in his hand, tilted slightly over his glass and waiting to pour its contents into the receptacle. "I don't recall telling you that. That's privileged information, and you didn't have the privilege."

"There's a lot of things you don't recall telling me," Johnny said. Robert made to say something, but Johnny put up a silencing hand. "It was Elmore who told me about Sheriff Lieber. You do remember telling the boy to start digging around on Mike to help you deal with him? He must've broke into your encrypted files and discovered your secret. I gotta give it to him—he was a sharp cookie to have figured it out. Part of me wishes that I hadn't bumped him off. He could've proved useful to me."

Robert shook his head, his eyes wide as saucers. "I should have never hired you," he said solemnly. "Mike proved himself capable before the sore spot he put me in; despite the blemish to his record I could still hold him in admirable regard. You, on the other hand...you were always a thorn on my side. You're just another incompetent underling, threatening to ruin everything I built like all the other incompetent underlings I have working for me now."

Johnny couldn't help but laugh. "If you have so many incompetent people working for you, doesn't that just prove how incompetent you are?"

"You can consider yourself terminated!" Robert shouted, slamming the bottle on the desk and shattering it. Vodka and glass went all over the place.

Johnny was unfazed. "Just as soon as you pay me a severance package for my years of dedicated service, I'll be out of your hair."

"Oh, so you want a severance package?" Robert asked. He gave Johnny a devilish grin as he walked back behind the desk and reached down under it. "Here, I think I have something that should satisfy you."

Before Robert could pull out the gun he had hidden in the opened safe under the desk, Johnny had already pulled out his gun and pointed it at his boss' chest. He fired three times, knocking Robert back into his chair with optimum force. Blood spewed on the back wall of the office as Robert dropped the gun to the floor and sprawled back in his chair, dead before he landed on the cushion of his seat.

Johnny holstered his gun and walked around the desk, pushing Robert and the chair out of the way as he looked beneath the desk. The door to the safe was open, revealing a few dozen envelopes full of cash. He smiled as he looked around the office until he found an empty box off to the side; he grabbed this and began stuffing the envelopes inside it.

Once he had everything in order he turned to his dead boss and tipped his hat to him.

"It was a pleasure doing business with you," Johnny said. "May I see you when I reach the scorched gates of the lake of fire Mister Christopher. Tell Lucifer I said hello."

This done, Johnny walked out of the office, out of the building, and out into the street where he parked his newly painted Jeep Wrangler.

Having killed the boss of one of the biggest crime syndicates along the eastern region of the country—and his immediate boss no less—Johnny could feel the overwhelming weight of a very dark future dragging along before him. Now he was on the run, and without so much as a partner to cover him Johnny felt absolutely alone. He would have to try and get a hold of Mike soon and beg him for forgiveness; though the bonds of friendship were a little more than strained at this point, Johnny figured he could still reason with him if given the chance.

These thoughts bounced around in his head as Johnny climbed into the Jeep and set the box full of money-stuffed envelopes on the passenger seat. He stuck the key in the ignition and started the engine; then as he felt the signs of doom and gloom starting to fade from him, Johnny did the unusual thing of buckling himself in.

A seatbelt might not do much good, but until he can reach his former partner Johnny figured he had better take all the safe bets from here on out.

CH. 22: MIKE'S CHANGE IN PLANS

Mike rose from his new lady's bed before the sun rose up and covered the morning sky. He could feel the strange mixture of beer and sensual delight swimming around in his head as he grabbed his pants from off the floor and slid into them. Doing this he quietly left from the room, taking a quick look back to Julia lying under her sheets, soundly and beautifully asleep from the hours she spent embracing something new and yet also familiar. Mike gave her a few moments' notice before shutting the door behind him and walking out into the hall.

The games that were played during the twilight moments of the night were the kind of games Mike had always loved to play, but this time they took on a more ominous hue as he engaged in the fiery depths of human anatomy and coupling. It wasn't guilt or religious preoccupation which had clouded Mike's mind; the thing that had begun to plague him was the sense that something was about to shift in focus fin his mind. Change was just within reach, touching him from somewhere in the horizon—Mike couldn't quite put a finger on it, but it loomed over him all the same: whispering inaudible words of comfort and longing, the likes of which had been gone from Mike since late adolescence. had brought with it the flickering glimpses of puppy love.

Mike considered this tidal wave of emotion as he came to the end of the hall and stood at the fork in the house, dividing the rustic decoration of the living room from the industrial efficiency of the kitchen. He took a few moments to stretch his legs before turning into the kitchen, making a beeline for the cupboards that stood directly over the coffee maker. He opened the cupboard and dug around until he had a container of Folger's brand coffee in hand; he took this as well as one of the filters from out of the pack, and then he closed the cupboard door shut.

Setting the container of coffee grounds on the counter, Mike opened the top of the coffee maker and placed the filter inside. He then grabbed a spoon from the silverware holder in the dish rack and used it to dip some of the grounds into the filter. He had the filter to about two-thirds full of grounds before he closed the lid on the container and set the spoon in the sink. He grabbed the empty pot and held it under the faucet of the sink; he turned on the cold water and watched it fill the pot to three-quarters before shutting off the running water and bringing the pot back to the maker. He opened the back lid of the maker and poured the water inside, feeling an odd fascination to the clear stream splashing into the bottom of the bin. Once the back of the maker was filled with water Mike closed the lid and placed the pot back in its original place.

All that was left to do was to make sure that the cord was plugged into the wall socket, which Mike did, and to press the ON button and let the coffee make itself, which Mike also did. The process took no more than five minutes, though it could have taken an hour or longer with the way that Mike had lost himself to the process.

Running on autopilot like he was, Mike might as well have been sleepwalking.

Mike stood by the counter and watched the coffee until it was done percolating, at which point he went to another cupboard and dug around until he found a mug that was big enough to satisfy his eye. He brought this over to the counter and grabbed the pot, filled to three-quarters, and poured the fresh black liquid gold into the mug till it steamed at nearly the inner rim of the cup. He then set the pot back into the docking station, brought the mug to his lips, and drank heavily.

It's not as good as Coke, Mike thought to himself, swallowing. *But I reckon it will have to do for now. Maybe Julia will go to the store later tonight and pick up a couple packs of canned soda. Then maybe we can go out dancing. That would be good enough for a first date I guess.*

The thought of first dates gave Mike pause to reflect on a few things. Considering that they were both in their thirties, and also considering what they'd done in the late hours of the night—in her own bed no less—it all made the idea of courtship seem stupid and a tad pointless. For all Mike's ability to charm the ladies, there was still a lot that he didn't know in terms of romance, chivalry, and the ways of the world. These were among the things that could have been taught to him by a proper father figure. And despite the one or two good people who guided him during his time at the orphanage, as well as the one or two people who gave tidbits of advice along the way after that, Mike never had much in the way of father figures. He didn't even know who his real father was, and there was a good chance that he would never know.

And for the life of him Mike couldn't figure why the issue of his parentage would chose to enter into his thoughts, here and now. All he could do once it came was to shake it out of his head as he walked over to the kitchen table, drinking his coffee as he eased himself into one of the chairs. From his seat he began to look out the window for whatever clues can be found in the morning sun, coming in to shine her light over the land and sea.

The more Mike looked out the window, the more he

wondered about all sorts of things—not the least of which was how he'd handle his life from here on out. He knew that he would again have to deal with his old boss eventually, and a part of him wanted to get it over with sooner rather than later. But as much as he knew he would have to handle the man who at one time acted as a father figure to him, Mike also knew that to run against Robert would mean to run against half the police and governmental orgs in the state. That was something that Mike would rather avoid.

If only Johnny were here with him now so Mike could go over ideas with him and figure this whole mess out. If only Johnny hadn't betrayed him for God knows why, when their boss was becoming more and more unglued as time wore on. With the way the world was crumbling around him, Mike Liebowitz could use the help of a good friend in this time of upheaval, desperation and need. As it stood all Mike could claim to have—was nothing.

Mike drained the rest of his coffee and went back to the counter to refill his mug. Once he refilled it he had a thought—and then he quickly set the mug and the pot on the counter and turned around, making a beeline for the living room. He found Julia's landline setting on a stand next to the couch; he looked down the hall to ensure that Julia was still asleep in the bedroom before walking over and picking it up. He dialed some numbers and held the receiver to his ear, listening to it ring until a whiny masculine voice picked up.

"Williams speaking," said the voice. "Who is this?"

"This is Mike," said Mike.

"Mike? As in Big Mike? Of Christopher's outfit? My God, I haven't heard from you in a while. I didn't recognize the number neither."

"Yeah, I borrowed a young lady's phone," Mike said. "Listen, do you think you can set me up for a trip out of the country? I might need to lay low for a few months. Spent the last couple of days just fiddling around, and that's not helping my situation any. Got anything for Mexico you need me to work for you? I swear I won't cut in for more than fifteen percent."

"That's a heck of a better deal than your boss would try and push me for," Williams answered. "The truth is I don't do much with the Mexican market anymore. But I can do you in for a job I got coming up in Quebec. How's your French?"

"It's not great," Mike admitted.

"Well no matter. I could still use a man of your skills for the job. That is, if you don't pull a stunt like you did with the car incident."

"Believe me," Mike said, "I want to put that and everything else behind me. I don't plan on screwing up on this."

"Well that's good," Williams said. "But what about your boss? You sure that Christopher ain't gonna have something to say about this?"

"I'm not working for Christopher anymore," Mike said curtly.

"Ok then," Williams answered. "That's understood I guess. The only other thing is this Mike. The job is really kind of a two-person thing. You and Johnny still tight? I could use his skills on this gig too, and the two of you work about as good as any two-man group I ever saw."

Mike grimaced but answered like he wasn't feeling a hundred shades of uncomfortable. "I can make a call just as soon as I get off the phone with you. Consider us both on the job."

"That's great," Williams said. "The job starts in a month. That ought to give you time to settle anything you got to settle before running this thing. Have Johnny call me and we'll finish everything up. And Mike? Thanks for calling me. You really helped me out."

"You too man," Mike answered. "You're giving me

another chance at life."

"What was that?" Williams asked.

"Nothing," Mike said. "I'll talk with you later." And with that Mike hung up, inspecting the receiver for several moments of careful reflection.

Mike struggled with making this next call. He figured on having to talk with Johnny again at some point, but to do it so soon made him feel restless. The fact was that Mike needed Johnny, now more than ever—but Johnny served a part in damaging him with the old boss, so there was that to consider as well. These rampant and disparate thoughts clustered around in Mike's head, threatening to drown him in their misery.

He could hear Julia stirring around in the bedroom, so he knew he'd better make things quick. He went ahead and called Johnny's cell, feeling the rush of adrenaline pump his blood through his veins with the speed of a high-powered locomotive.

After a few rings Johnny picked up. "Hello? Who's this?"

"It's me Johnny," Mike said.

"Oh," Johnny said, after a moment's pause. "I didn't recognize the number."

"Yeah, about that. I had a little bit of phone trouble in the last day or so."

"Is that right?"

"Yeah. Listen, I just spoke to Williams. He says he has a job for us in Canada. Starts in a month if you're interested."

"A job in Canada huh? That might be interesting this time of year."

"Yeah, it might. So what do you say? Are you in?"

"Sure, I got no plans."

"What about the boss?"

"Don't worry about him. I quit last night, and managed to get a good amount of severance pay along with it. I reckon it's enough for us to split down the middle. I owe you that much at least."

"Well that's good," Mike said, not without some reservation. He fell silent for a moment to choke down a soft cry, managed to pull himself together, and then said, "Look Johnny, I should've called you back yesterday when I had the chance. Everything came to a head, and I was in a sore mess, and I couldn't make out anything without coming undone—"

"Don't sweat it Mike," Johnny said. "We have plenty of time to work it out while in Canada. Is there a chance I can catch up with you beforehand? There's some stuff I think you ought to know."

"Sure, just come on down to Virginia Beach. I found a sweet spot to hang for a while. We can take care of everything here."

"Sounds good Mike. Give me an address and I'll make my way there later in the day."

Mike gave him an address and set up a time to meet. At this point he could hear Julia call out to him from the bedroom. "Mike? What are you doing out there? Did you make coffee?"

"I'll be with you in a minute," Mike called out to her. He drew his attention back to Johnny on the phone. "Sorry about that. I'll see you later on ok?"

"No problem Mike," Johnny said. "And Mike? I'm sorry too. I've had my share of stuff come up just like you did, and I don't like it much at all. Maybe when I tell you about it we can make some sense of it together."

"Maybe we can," Mike said. "In any case I'll see you later."

"Yeah, I'll see you. And then in a month, we'll be in Canada."

"Yep, in a month."

"See you in a few Mike. Take care for now."

"Same to you Johnny. Bye."

Mike hung up the phone and walked back into the

kitchen, grabbing his mug and drawing it to his lips. He stopped to look out the window again, catching sight of the sun rising to her fresh morning spot and stretching out her arms before the cosmos. She shone brightly this morning, showcasing the finer points of her majesty and beauty. Mike took a look at her, and he smiled.

"This is as good as it gets I reckon," he said, and then he set the mug down and made for the bedroom. He only had a month in which to take part in this sordid affair, and he wanted to get the most out of it.

THE END

GHOSTS AT THE DOOR
A BONUS STORY

Nobody bothered to ask Joe Hill how he felt about his momma's death, but Joe Hill was the one needing to be asked the most. Martha Bradley, being the pompous, forever old-looking gossip that she was, liked to impose her wild speculations on Joe every now and again (gossips need their interrogations the way that true believers need the security of their religion), but the first time she came down to the shop and made Joe stop changing Old Man Carter's tires on his Jeep and told him about what kinds of pills are available for post-mortem depression, Joe Hill let out a cussing fit the likes of which he hadn't put forth in over fifteen years. Joe rarely ever got so mad, and he hardly even spoke to his friends while out drinking or while out living his life in general; but that Bradley woman got hold of him on a bad day, and in a dark frame of mind.

Half the shop fell into a riot over the way that Joe made Martha look like a fool. A good time was had by all.

After the blowup down at the shop, still nobody asked Joe how he felt about his momma—a woman no one could even remember seeing much more than a few moments here and there during her short walks to school, wearing her summer coat and her worn out slippers—and the fact that she up and died suddenly, just like that sure raised a lot of questions. After the shop Martha Bradley tried her best to stir the pot around town and sink Joe's name right down the toilet. Gossips hate it when the face of humiliation turns and starts paying them a mind, but this ole girl was having no luck at all in her pursuits. Though nobody could be bothered to pry into their friend's business (when prying could've probably done the most damn good), enough of the citizens of Flat Rock liked Joe to know that he was a man simply having a fit over losing his dear old mother, a woman nobody even saw much of for more than a few moments here and there, in her threadbare slippers and summer jacket.

They figured that Joe was simply in the beginning stages of mourning. If they had only known what was coming up ahead, then they could have done something. It was only the one fit to begin with, and nobody could foresee a trend in the making.

But in church on Sunday morning Joe had another little fit—this time it was directed at the good Reverend Foster Green. Reverend Green simply asked the poor man how he was holding up considering.

"I'm holding up just fine, if anybody gives a d—!" Joe roared, and then he turned and flipped the reverend off in such a grand fashion as to cause the pianist Gertrude Cole to faint, her face landing right on the middle keys. It took three other parishioners half an hour to wake her up and get the old lady into a decent frame of mind.

Everybody that knew Joe (and there were quite many in Flat Rock who knew Joe Hill, whether by drinking with him down at the bar or by having him work on their cars) still liked the man well enough despite these outbursts; they saw Joe as a man who over the course of forty-three years proved not only to be a loyal son to a practical shut-in mother, but also a staple in their hometown. But the church incident made people a little uneasy going around a man they now considered to be a heater belt with a broken switch. Two major outbursts in a week—one of them in a church, no less—tend to leave people gun-shy so far as asking questions and making small talk in general is concerned. When they come up to the shop to get their cars worked on, they might talk about the weather, or if Coach Tyler at Wheatley High'll get those pea-brained Sprockets to shape up this season. But now mostly they just treaded on those eggshells piling up on the floor, wondering what in the hell had happened to their dear old friend Joe Hill.

The people continued to talk and to gossip, wondering if Joe should keep working or take a break, wondering if maybe a woman would do him some good, even wondering if talking to the man would mean something. It was all talk and nothing came of it.

The period between Nora Hill's death and her son Joe's second outburst down at the church totaled eight days. Nine and a half weeks later, Joe was found dead—he drove around in his prime Chevy step-side with the chrome wheels and the 8-ball on the stick shift, and raced head first into Mountain Goat Pond and drowned. Everything that could have happened in that time did happen, and the people involved felt like sorry culprits indeed.

This is the story of those nine and a half weeks.

>>>

For three of those nine weeks Joe moped about town going this way and that, with everybody who passed by him wondering whether they should step up and say something to him, anything, a kind word or maybe just a give-em-hell. He finally just left the shop in the capable hands of Harlan Modesitt, and he let the people draw their own conclusions without a word come out of anybody's mouth. The people were just as cautious of what Joe might do as they were scared for him.

The mayor liked to tell incoming visitors that in Flat Rock, *Everyone Cares for You*. But while the townspeople of Flat Rock did care for each other in the deepest possible way, for the most part they didn't much lift a finger to do anything about it. Least of all for Joe. People still liked to act all scared and catlike, behaving rather stupidly.

By the start of the fourth week Jack Haldeman's nine-year-old boy David started talking to Joe over shakes down at Pop's Pharmacy. After that first conversation, the two started palling around rather suddenly; they could just about always be seen going to or from Mountain Goat's Pond with their fishing poles and tackle boxes, along with a nice big ice chest filled with glass bottles of orange Nehi and Coke. This was of course during the extreme high spike in the summer, when the sun would beat down on men's backs with both fists clenched down hard, and everybody in Flat Rock had to chug on sweet tea or cold beer just to make it through the longer and longer days.

One day while the two were out fishing—after Joe caught himself two mudcats and David chanced on a striped bass—David asked Joe, "When you gonna finally cry over your momma, Mr. Hill?" He looked up at his friend, drinking a Nehi and shading his tired eyes from the bullying downpour of the sun's rays. His brows were dark and burrowed into their sockets; he had spent the night before reading comics he bought from the Pharmacy.

"I told you just to call me Joe, son," Joe declared, keeping his at-then sightless eyes straight ahead on the water. "And besides, ain't you one always saying men don't cry, no way no how?" He began to squeak out the weakest, most insincere laugh one could ever let out on a day like this, with summer lasting forever and the water so clear.

"That no-crying stuff's all bullsh— when your momma dies off," David said, polishing off the rest of his Nehi. Joe didn't even bother to scold the boy for cussing; after all it wasn't his job to raise the kid, and besides to cuss is to enter a doorway into manhood (by Joe's own humble estimation).

"Well, it can get kinda hard to cry over dead people,

David, if they were half dead already while they were livin'." Joe sighed, and told David to go on and pass him a Coke, "And for God's sake cast yer line out already—that one mudcat you caught won't enough to crack a pebble."

They both laughed, and it was a good, wholesome, genuine laugh at that.

>>>

Lorna stood in the kitchen preparing dinner. With Joe Hill coming over pretty regular now the food was taking on a higher quality—Lorna could still remember their high school days together, the love that was made and the nights that were spent out in the bed of Joe's truck listening to George Strait hits on the radio. Lorna figured one of these nights to play a new George Strait tape she bought at the convenience store during the meal, just to see if it would juggle up any memories for Joe like it did for her. With an old flame suddenly entering the picture, Lorna felt like she could start a wildfire—why she should care after so many years she didn't know, but it sure felt good to remember it all.

Jack came in from work and saw his wife working on a grand feast. He let a smile creep up on his face as he inched over and put his arms around Lorna, making to kiss her on the neck. But Lorna shrieked, scared as if being attacked, and leapt out of her dear husband's grasp.

Jack couldn't believe it. "Hey now, what gives? I come home every night and hug and kiss you—tonight you act like it's the end of the world and I'm a stranger. What's wrong with you?"

Lorna collected herself and went back to her work, barely even looking at her husband. "Nothing's wrong. I just didn't hear you come in and I was startled. Nothing to it really."

Jack watched as his wife continued with the dinner preparations. As he did he noticed an extra place set at the kitchen table, and he grew a little heated. "I see we're having your old boyfriend over again. How cute; when are we gonna stop with this same old argument Lorna?"

Lorna turned and gave her husband a cautious glance. "Cool it Jack, our son happens to like him—"

"And I don't like that either. It's unnatural for a nine-year-old to be hanging around with a man older than you or me. Why can't he have a friend his own age?"

"You run off every child he brings around the house to play with," Lorna said flatly, beginning to place the food out on the table. "I swear I ain't never seen a man more scared of children laughing and playing in my whole life."

Jack snorted, waving her off as he went to the fridge looking for a beer. "Dumb kids make too much noise. I work 50 to 60 hours a week down at the clothing factory, and dammit all when I come home it's not too much to want some peace around here." He swiped a couple of bottles from the refrigerator door, brought them over and sat down at the head of the table. He kept on muttering to himself, as though there weren't a soul else in the room to talk to.

Lorna continued working on dinner, shaking her head to herself. In truth, she was glad to have Joe back in her life, and she was doubly so to have him take an interest in her son. Though Jack sorely loved David, as a father he was only a mediocre product; the fact that he worked so much didn't help with matters. There have been a couple of nights where she laid awake long hours at a time, thinking about her old-school days in the arms of a man who was not her husband. More than once during these times she wept silently to herself so as not to disturb the man who was asleep beside her. The memories were just so raw and palpable, so vivid and real, so damnedly not going to come back again in this life, that Lorna felt the urge just to leave everything behind. The urge was getting harder to ignore every day.

As Lorna finished putting together the food (with a full

plate on her mind), Jack felt an urge within himself to instigate some stuff. "What you know about Joe's momma baby?"

Lorna didn't bat an eye at the question. "Oh lord Jack, I haven't seen much of her in over 20 years. I'm the last person to ask about Joe Hill's momma."

"They say she was crazy as a loon, had to see a shrink just to maintain even a little bit." Jack added a wry little smile, and added, "Don't you find that interesting?"

Lorna pursed her lips and finished setting the table, not even looking at her husband. "No, I don't think that's interesting Jack. I don't want to get too deep into the lives led by dead people."

"No, you just want to get back into the pants of the live ones." Jack snorted again.

Lorna didn't say a word; she stormed out of the kitchen ready to tear the walls down from their support beams. Jack could be heard laughing through the house, casually drinking his beer as a reward for a job well done.

And as angry as Lorna was she could not deny that the seed of curiosity had been planted in her mind. Joe Hill had been good to her in the past, but his mother had kept them apart. Perhaps there was something to what her bastard husband was saying, something worth considering. With the weight of residual love—or maybe lust—trafficking in her soul, Lorna wanted to walk the earth to satisfy her mind's probing questions.

Perhaps it was time to get out of the house more and figure this all out.

>>>

At somewhere between five and six weeks, a man named Dr. Lainard tooled on in to Flat Rock, driving a big luxury SUV. He drove over to Joe's place and started staying over there for a bit. After the doctor appeared the only people within town to see Joe Hill with any regularity were David and David's family—the boy practically begged that they keep going down to the water for bass-slaying, gutting them out and taking them back to David's place for a grand supper with the rest of the Haldeman bunch. Lorna, Jack Haldeman's wife and David's mother, was always kind of sweet on Joe and she let it be known every time he came over. They used to be high school lovers, Joe and Lorna, before Joe's momma started demanding more and more of his time and Lorna got on with Jack after they had broken away from each other. Jack Haldeman was a special sort of jealous over the two of them; Joe and Lorna seemed to channel energies left over from the bleachers in the gym and the pep rallies like there wasn't a thing to it.

After the hour or so of the evening meal had finished, and Joe ended his round of stupid jokes with the kid, Joe would gather his rod and tackle and head for home (where a certain Dr. Lainard took to staying). Out in the thick of the town, people began to gossip.

Martha Bradley had done some digging around on Lainard, and found that the man was a well-respected therapist and professor of psychology at some small college over the hill from Flat Rock (the same small college where Joe took an English degree he didn't use because of his mother) and he had Nora Hill under his care for quite an extensive amount of time. Once the gossip hound's nose picked up a prickly scent, Martha started preaching hellfire on Joe to all her friends she'd cultivated over the years just for this purpose. Within four days the whole town of Flat Rock was set ablaze, with questions as to whether Good Joe Hill and his mother Nora were...well, kind of funny in the mental arena.

Eyes were shifting about the place. Word went this place and that. Time was no longer a precious commodity to be spent carefully, but rather a cheap fluid thing to be flung out with the bath water and the scraps for dogs.

Time was fast approaching the seven-week marker, and people started seeing Dr. Lainard walking about town all by himself, frequenting the Tastee Freeze for burgers and shakes. On one particular occasion, Lainard was eating on a Big T Burger with a fork and knife, even going so far as to fork up his ketchup-drenched fries to keep his precious soft hands from getting salt and condiments all over them (thus keeping his obsessive-compulsive world intact). The man looked so devilishly out of place that everybody swore they were just seeing things every time they looked his way. Some of the old barflies drinking their coffee decided to put away the nightly beer runs for a while; they thought they were seeing things too and they were getting superstitious.

It was here at the Tastee Freeze, where they were taking a trip for their regular chocolate milkshake binge, that Lorna and David saw Dr. Lainard for the first time to speak of. The mother and her son each silently agreed to go over and make conversation—Lorna wanted to get a handle on the doctor, and David wanted to find a way to get his fishing buddy back on the right track. Joe was starting to get a little weird lately down at the pond, talking more and more nonsense the few times he did speak each trip that they took together.

"Hello Doctor Lainard," Lorna stated, reaching out her hand in a feigned neighborly attempt at a handshake. Lainard took her hand graciously (almost too graciously for such an ordinary meeting), and after a bit he took David's hand as well. With these formalities out of the way, Lorna asked, "May we sit here with you?"

Lainard affirmed her request with a light nod and a grand sigh, and Lorna ushered David into the empty end of the scratched-out booth. Lainard followed them in seating himself, and then the three of them sat there awkwardly for what seemed like a stretched-out eternity (stretched out beyond reason, beyond form, beyond need). People scattered around dining in were craning their necks to catch glances their way, wanting to get the scoop on what was going on at the lonely little booth up against the sunlit window.

Finally, in an effort to break the tension that was causing him obvious discomfort, Lainard cleared his throat and said, "In my profession, ma'am, bouts of silence that go on this long are never considered a good thing." He tried at a friendly smile, and added, "Is there anything I can do for you, Missus...?"

"*Miss* Lorna Haldeman, Doctor Lainard—I know full well who you are. This here is my son David." David wanted to correct his mama, say that she actually was a *missus*; the boy in some small way sorely loved his daddy Jack, and he didn't fully understand why his own mother would want to pose off as someone who was single when she was in fact a married woman. She had even taken off her wedding band.

But before David could utter more than a syllable, Lorna hushed him and swatted his hand down. She had strong feelings leading her sudden curiosity, and she was going to follow those feelings down into hell if she had to, wedding vows be damned.

"Well, *Miss* Haldeman, you can call me Philip if you'd please. Doctor Lainard is much too formal in a place such as this. Excuse me for just a moment..." Lainard rose and took his tray off to the trash, having finished most of his meal and deciding he was too full to stow away the rest. He threw the paper and food away separately; then he decided to take his tray up to the counter instead of leaving it on the allotted space overtop the can.

Upon returning Lainard made a little drama of sitting down, and he asked, "Now again, is there anything at all I can do for you and your son today?" He gave David a little wink and a grin, which almost made David lose his shake and some of his breakfast from that morning.

"Well," Lorna started, lolling her eyes about as she tried desperately to word what she wanted to say. She tilted her head to the side and began to scratch her chin in such an exaggerated fashion that it almost started another reaction in her son, one more intensely than he felt close to coming on when Lainard winked at him. The way that the tension was building, the whole restaurant was close to having a reaction of one kind or another—for some it was a comedy, for others a soap opera. All were of valid concern here.

Lorna let the silence build just a little more, and then she said, "There's been a lot of talk going on about town, about a therapist stayin' over at Joe Hill's place. People say you treated his momma—is that true?"

She stared at Lainard with wild eyes, though that might've been unintentional. Lorna had wanted to show genuine concern, but she was never any good at subversive measure in revealing her intentions and moods to the men she encountered in her life. Her bedroom came to a screeching locked door with her husband because of this very problem.

"You should know of course that I cannot delve into my patients' problems, past or present, or the nature of my treatment with them," Lainard said, wringing mother and son for everything that they had. "Confidentiality can be a real pain in the ass—pardon my language—but I must oblige it nevertheless. Surely a lady of your keen senses and grace should understand my obligation…"

Lorna shot the man a cold, calculating glare, sharp enough to squeeze Lainard's head clean off if her eyes could but grow hands and reach out for the neck. She'd always hated being patronized by people with educations that neither she or her parents could afford to have for herself. "Doctor Lainard, around here we always know if someone's teenage girl gets pregnant—your wants of privacy are not important to me. I want information, and I want it now."

At this Lainard simply stood up and smiled down on Lorna and her son. "It is often hard for simple people to grasp anything beyond the simple." When Loran moved to protest at his insult, he put up a sweaty hand to stop her.

"Ma'am, let me assure you that your beau is more than well taken care of, as are the affairs of his mother. Let me see to him, and you just see to your little man here." He gave the boy another wink-and-grin combo.

David, creeped out beyond repair, had to excuse himself for the bathroom.

Dr. Lainard, in turn, excused himself for the soda fountain. He grabbed his cup, walked on over amid the stares coming from customers and employees alike. Lainard paid no mind to all the attention as he refilled his Cheerwine. He took a big swallow, bent down and added tea to his soda, and took another long and careful sip. Nodding to himself, he walked back towards the booth, stopping just before he made it out to the door. Standing over Lorna in a dominating fashion, he said, "You seem tense ma'am. How's your love life?"

Lorna promptly shot up out of her seat and slapped Lainard so hard across the face that everybody in the Tastee Freeze heard the man's teeth rattle inside his head. "If you aren't going to behave in a manner that is benign, then at least do me the courtesy and not act malign either. Kindly do both me and the world a favor. And drop dead." And with that Lorna collected her stuff as well as her son's, and she walked over to the bathroom to wait on David. Once he got out of the bathroom, they both left straight for home, with not another word spoken to anyone else inside of the restaurant. Everyone watched them go.

Everybody's attention soon diverted from the exiting mother and her child and towards Dr. Philip Lainard, left to stand there in the middle of the floor, clutching his tea and Cheerwine like it was a hundred percent gold. No breaths could be heard in the space of a minute.

Any other person made to suffer such embarrassment would at least blush the slightest at the humiliation. But Dr. Lainard was clearly not any other person put in such an embarrassing spot; he just pointed everybody out in the place and laughed at them all. "You're all so sick and you'd be beyond my help!" he shouted, and then he walked right out of the Tastee Freeze and climbed into his SUV, still laughing like crazy as he put the key in the ignition, cranked her up and began to drive off.

Among the shocked people left inside the restaurant was Martha Bradley, who spent the whole time in a small corner table watching everything go down between Lorna Haldeman and the new town visitor. She smiled as she snuck out of the place amid all the new gossip and got into her beat-up Pontiac to follow the not-so-good doctor the direction he was headed, all the way back to Joe's place.

>>>

Joe and David went out fishing again, this time amid a town wide chaos—what with the whole storm beginning to rain down on the entirety of Flat Rock, with a vile stench that was unsurpassed in most Southern towns (excluding Texas and Arkansas).

Martha Bradley was becoming the worst kind of gossip: the kind with a vengeance, and anyone with any sense could tell just by looking at her—but it took her standing right next to Dr. Lainard neck and neck before anyone could see that they were equals in some respects. She worked the man over so hard the day she followed him until he broke down and told her everything about Nora Hill's series of debilitating neuroses, which had permeated themselves into her son's life in more ways than one.

Dr. Lainard, defeated, clammed up and went back inside, not wanting to see his victor anymore forever. Clinging to the last bit of professionalism he had left he kept his mouth shut; but the venom was still sticking to his veins and he wished to let it out soon.

If the circumstances were different the two of them would have been lovers.

Martha could never get over Joe slighting her at the shop, so she decided to spread the word out amongst her inner circle, who then took to spreading said word out the rest of the way. Everybody in Flat Rock was all up in arms over this small but juicy bit of local news, want to know how Joe, their precious Joe Hill, was going to hold up considering such a revelation (none of them would go up and ask him outright).

Well as David sat there on the log next to Joe, fishing off the bank at Mountain Goat Pond, Joe had discovered upon an unspoken thought, maybe the only thought he had had on the whole matter—the thought of casual annoyance.

"Maybe we should just let that one go," Joe muttered, untangling his line from a piece of driftwood floating in the water.

"Momma's been getting all worked up trying to figure out all kinds of stuff she can do for you," David said, sucking down a root beer and watching on his line with what can only be described as mediocre vigilance at best. "Daddy keeps saying that she ought to have married you instead of marrying him. Then momma goes off and starts acting like it was all a big mistake." David belched, and then he added, "Sometimes I think momma's off her chain. She can be a real pill sometimes."

"You should be nicer to your mother, what with all the preaching you gave me the other day out here," Joe said, poking his friend at the side with his elbow, a huge grin painted on his face. He was eating out of a big bag of UTZ Salt and Vinegars, licking the salt off his fingers after every other handful.

"Why, heck, Joe—you know how much I love my momma, but the truth's the truth and it's gotta be said. She's downright off her chain!" Both Joe and David laughed their hind quarters off, slapping their knees and snorting like hogs. When they finally calmed themselves back down, David said, "That Doctor Lainard looks like some carnival freak, you know. We saw him at the Tastee Freeze the other day, and he wouldn't stop winking at me—it was just plain weird."

"Phil Lainard is a billy bastard who likes to call everybody else a billy bastard so that he don't have to feel so bad." Both boy and man went back to laughing at that one, and for that moment in that afternoon the world outside of Mountain Goat Pond was just a far-off figment of the imagination, and one that was only half-imagined at that. The sun was just getting ready to set behind the earth, acting as a sort of punctuation to the day's sentence.

"Martha Bradley is mighty sore at you," David remarked, as a quick tug hit at his line.

"Yep," Joe said, "maybe she and the doctor should be together and get it over with. Ain't neither one of them able to nab a spouse; they deserve each other." It was as funny as anybody could make spur-of-the-moment, but neither Joe nor David got a chance to laugh, because by then David had trouble reeling in whatever it was tugging at his line. Both of them worked for a solid dime hauling her in, taking what looked to be a nine or ten pound mudcat from the water. They both cheered as loud as they could, high-fiving each other at the good supper they'd have that night along with the rest of David's messed-up family.

This all took place at about eight and a half weeks.

>>>

Lorna wouldn't talk to Jack for days—she was too angered to even see straight. At times, she thought of killing her husband, but she always quickly brushed the idea aside as not very practical.

Jack took to drinking more and more—a lot of men in Flat Rock drank too much, and Jack already had a reputation for an overly healthy appetite. Things were going bad in the Haldeman household, and something was about to go down.

Joe Hill could feel a stirring in his bones that he couldn't even describe. He was itching for a fight and couldn't put a finger on who to pounce on until finally it all came together towards the end and a body just had to go and do it, consequences be damned.

The night before Joe was to be found dead and fit to be buried, he drove over to Jack Haldeman's house. Lorna and David had gone to see her mom for the weekend, and there was not a spare soul to be had to share in what was to come about. This was to be two men hashing things out, things which had until now been left unsaid. They were going to be said on this night however, and they weren't going to be said lightly.

Joe walked right into the house by the front door, found Jack drinking at the kitchen table and reading the paper. Jack looked up and nodded in acknowledgement of his new house guest. The room was silent for several minutes.

Finally, Jack cleared his throat. "That Doctor Lainard said some not so kind things to my wife."

"Yeah I heard," said Joe. "He won't be staying at my house too long."

"That's good to hear. Now what do you want?"

"I want Lorna, that's what I want."

Jack looked up from the paper, picked up his beer and took a drink as he eyed Joe coolly. "Think you can handle a woman who mothered a kid, can you? Momma's boy like you trying to get out from under a shadow and live a little bit..."

"My momma's been long gone. Shut up."

Jack laughed. "Do what you came here to do man. I ain't gonna waste no more time on you." He drank some more of his beer and looked down at his paper.

Joe didn't waste any time either. He rushed Jack and grabbed him by the collar, pulling him out of his chair and pummeled him into the ground. Beer and newsprint went everywhere; the sight was hard to follow for several minutes.

By the time he finally let up Joe straightened and went into the fridge in the pantry where Jack kept all his beer. It took him three trips to get all the cases he wanted, and then before he left he stepped back in to get a glimpse of the body and soul, the remains of body and soul he left out on the kitchen floor.

"I've done grown up now Jack. Best just let it all go."

And with that the victor went back to the truck, cranked her up, slammed the door shut and drove off, Waylon Jennings singing "Mona Lisa Lost Her Smile" on the radio and the beer cold as Joe grabbed one up and opened her. He drank as he drove, and the night seemed to open up to him without any trouble.

This was the night before there was to be any trouble, and not a care was given anywhere in the world. Not on this night, not under this moon.

At nine and a half weeks, Joe Hill drove his truck down into Mountain Goat Pond and drowned to death—there wasn't even a sign that he'd tried to get out of the cab. When the tow truck pulled her out the police found a half-ton of empty beer bottles and cans up in the can with Joe.

Dr. Lainard said before he left that it was a form of self-medicating—it was one of the few things people caught on to before they decided to kick the man out of town three or four days later for being such an arrogant nuisance. David watched the man leave town, half expecting him to start calling people billy bastards—but of course he never did.

Even as he drove out of town Lainard behaved like he owned the place—he'd probably still carry that attitude with him until time for the devil to decide to take him down below.

Reverend Green had the hardest time performing the funeral, standing before what ended up being the largest crowd he ever had inside the church walls. A man of grace once he had time to think, the reverend suddenly felt sorry for pestering Joe that day, before so much hell had gone down the drain for them all. He cried his way through the eulogy, as did half the church.

At the end of the service, when it came time for one last viewing of the body, David came up with his mother and set and empty Nehi bottle inside the casket with Joe's body. he whispered a few sorrowful words over the loss of his fishing buddy. But he didn't do any crying over the casket—Lorna did enough of that for the both of them.

Jack Haldeman wasn't with the rest of his family at the funeral; he was still healing over the wounds inflicted in what some would call a fight, others would call an all-out assault. He left Lorna to cry over her old flame and returned to her sister Beth who was his old flame—she was more than ready to take him back into her arms, even if it were only for a little while until the dust settled for a bit.

One of the other people not at the funeral was the deposed queen Martha Bradley—after Joe died and people began feeling heartsick, nobody took any stock in anything the woman had to say anymore (they'd had enough venom in their lives). This left her without a friend in the world, and it would probably stay that way for a good long while.

Martha Bradley wasn't in any good frame of mind to go to the funeral anyway; soon it would be known all about Flat Rock via her old circle of comrade that she and Dr. Lainard had in fact "gotten together" like Joe had predicted. They got together a handful of times, two people oddly attracted to each other by their mutual arrogance; and after he'd had his fun Lainard had decided it was high time to leave—with an unexpected little gift growing inside of her.

And so, Joe Hill, considered a good man and a staple in Flat Rock, had died. Leaving Flat Rock's citizens trying desperately to keep things as close to the old ways as they could. But it would never be the same, not while everybody still among the living had to keep fighting the ghosts at the door. May God have mercy on their souls.

"And God shall wipe away all tears from their eyes; and

there shall be no more death, neither sorrow, nor crying, neither shall there be any more pain: for the former things are passed away." *Revelation 21:4, King James Version*

ABOUT THE AUTHOR

James Lawson Moore is a poet and wannabe screenwriter originally from the city of Richmond, Virginia. After studying English at Regent University, he now happily divides his time between Virginia Beach and Chesterfield. This is his first novel; he plans to write many other crime and thriller novels along the way, while sustaining himself on a steady diet of coffee and cheeseburgers.

You can reach James in the regular online haunts and hang-outs, including Twitter. Just look for the handle @soggybottompoet. His Facebook page is under the banner "James Moore, the Wannabe Artist".